THE INCREDIBLE DIARY OF...

Amazing Stories

Edited By Briony Kearney

First published in Great Britain in 2024 by:

 Young**Writers**® Est. 1991

Young Writers
Remus House
Coltsfoot Drive
Peterborough
PE2 9BF
Telephone: 01733 890066
Website: www.youngwriters.co.uk

Printed and bound in the UK by BookPrintingUK
Website: www.bookprintinguk.com
YB0MA0041A

Foreword

Dear Diary,

You will never guess what I did today! Shall I tell you? Some primary school pupils wrote some diary entries and I got to read them, and they were EXCELLENT!

Here at Young Writers we created some bright and funky worksheets along with fun and fabulous (and free) resources to help spark ideas and get inspiration flowing. And it clearly worked because WOW!! I can't believe the adventures I've been reading about. Real people, make-believe people, dogs and unicorns, even objects like pencils all feature and these diaries all have one thing in common – they are JAM-PACKED with imagination!

Here at Young Writers we want to pass our love of the written word onto the next generation and what better way to do that than to celebrate their writing by publishing it in a book! It sets their work free from homework books and notepads and puts it where it deserves to be – OUT IN THE WORLD!

Each awesome author in this book should be SUPER PROUD of themselves, and now they've got proof of their imagination, their ideas and their creativity in black and white, to look back on in years to come!

Contents

Cadder Primary School, Glasgow

LaToya Micheal (9)	28
Pearl Lin (9)	29
Terrence Gao (10)	30
Precious Izogie (9)	31
Shay Mclaren (10)	32
Ava Kelly (10)	33
Valeria Gamboa (10)	34
Harper Omnet (9)	35

Cannington CE Primary School, Cannington

Simion Sauca (9)	36

Chantry Middle School, Morpeth

Izzy Pringle (11)	37
Imogen Blewett (11)	38
Annabella Huxley (11)	40
Emily Havis (11)	42
Grace Bell (12)	44
Charlotte Burn (11)	46
Joshua Towers (11)	48
Charlie Rutherford (11)	50
Mason Blight (11)	51
Alexa Hedley (11)	52
Jude Danby (10)	53

Christ The King Catholic Primary School, Stockton-On-Tees

Emily Ions (10)	54

Claycots School, Slough

Muhammad Mustafaul Haque (8)	56
Maryam Babne (9)	57

Comely Park Primary School, Falkirk

Olivia Wood Rose (10)	58

Coteford Junior School, Eastcote

Millie-Mae Lupton (9)	60

Cowley St Laurence CE Primary School, Cowley

Aathira Sutharsan (8)	61
Nidha Ann Saju (8)	62

Cradlehall Primary School, Westhill

Ewan Fraser (10)	63
Kourtney Mackenzie (9)	64

D H Christie Memorial Primary School, Coleraine

Rocco Freeman (9)	66
Danny Doherty (9)	68

Eastern Green Junior School, Coventry

Isla Ferguson (9)	69
Bailey Dalton (8)	70
Boaz Ibitoye (9)	71
Danny Turner (9)	72
Georgia Gibbs (9)	73

Edgbaston High School For Girls, Edgbaston

Amelia Haywood (9)	74
Hitha Inamadugu (8)	76
Haaniya Sabir (9)	77
Aditi Mohanraj (10)	78
Ariane Li (9)	79
Ruth Li (8)	80

Edward Worlledge Ormiston Academy, Great Yarmouth

Effie Smalldridge (9)   81

Emneth Academy, Emneth

Kasia Snopek (8)   82

Farfield Primary & Nursery School, Bradford

Kelsey-Leigh Greenhough (10)	83
Lily Kelley (9)	84
Ellie-Jo Cawley (9)	86
David Cenuse (9)	88
Kyen Whitaker (9)	90

Fir Tree Primary School & Nursery, Newbury

William Banning (10)	92
Ruby Draper (10)	93

Grafton Primary School, Holloway

Salma Khatun (8)	94
Amelie Malach (8)	96
Safiyah Ahmed (8)	98
Ceyda Kaygusuz (8)	99
Niaz Miah (7)	100
Ridwan Ibrahim (8)	101
Jaylen Carrera (8)	102

Greenfield Primary School, Stourbridge

Gideon Adams (9)   103

Grosvenor Road Primary School, Swinton

Chloe Ainsworth (9)	104
Mohammed Gabralla (9)	106

Hartlebury CE Primary School, Hartlebury

Jasmine Holmes (9)   107

Highgate Primary Academy, Goldthorpe

Zoe Nyerges (9)	108
Georgia Browning (9)	109
Phoebe Deakin (8)	110
Isabella Frost (10)	111
Beau-James Ash (9)	112
Noah Mallinson (9)	113

Holbrook Primary School, Bridgemary

Mia Franklin (10)	114
Caelyn Lane (10)	115

Holy Family Catholic Primary School, West Acton

Matthew Trzcinski (11)   116

Hopton Primary School, Hopton

Zoe Vaughan (8)	117
Ellina Gooda (8)	118

Hunsbury Park Primary School, Camp Hill

Frank Grzela (9)	119
Andrew Lazar (8)	120
Kofi Ofosu Sarpong (8)	121
Nicola Krusinsku (10)	122
Amelia Bell (9)	123

Kettins Primary School, Kettins

Esme Murray (11)   124

Kimbolton St James' CE Primary School, Kimbolton

Henry Rayner (8)   126

Kingsmoor Primary School, Bawdrip

Alisha Addicott (8)   127

Knockmore Primary School, Lisburn

Kasie-Leigh Anderson (9)   128

Lakes Primary School, Redcar

Finley Huseltine (10)   129

Langtree Community School, Langtree

Rosie Rayner (11)   130
Chester Taylor-Coleman (10)   131

Laughton Junior & Infant School, Laughton-En-Le-Morthen

Brax Pritchard (9)   132

Margaretting CE (VC) Primary School, Margaretting

Demie Smith (10)   133

Mayfield Preparatory School, Walsall

Aadam Azeem (9)   134
Aydin Shan (9)   135

Mill Lodge Primary School, Shirley

Kyle Deeble (10)   136
Lucas Moss (8)   138
Luca Cox (9)   139

Millquarter Primary School, Toomebridge

Sinéad Hannon (9)   140
Orla McGrogan (9)   142

Moredon Primary & Nursery School, Moredon

Simisola Amusa (9)   143

Muscliff Primary School, Bournemouth

Frankie Little (10)   144

North Petherton Community Primary School, North Petherton

Sonny Mee (10)   145
Isla Cole (10)   146
Liliana B (11)   148
Mason Nixon (10)   150

Outwood Primary Academy Bell Lane, Ackworth

Lilly-Mae Fox (9)   151

Pelsall Village School, Pelsall

Max Roberts (10)   152

Queen's Park Primary School, Westminster

Fatimah Zeidan (10)   153

Riverside Primary School, Barking

Layla Omar (11)   154

Rosedale Primary School, Hayes

Anjali Raithatha (9)   155
Matias Baintan (10)   156
Yasmin Islam (10)   157

Samares Primary School, St Clement

Harrison Parker Leitch (8)   158

Sculthorpe CE Primary School, Sculthorpe

Bethany Norman (8)   159

Seaton School, Aberdeen

Kayla Derrett (9)   160

Southmuir Primary School, Kirriemuir

Noah Duncan (11)   161

St Andrew's CE Primary School, Whitmore Reans

Awais Ali (10)   162

St Brigid's Primary School, Londonderry

Abigail Starrs (9)   163
Priya McEmerson (9)   164
Dean McIntyre (9)   165

St Edward's Catholic Primary School, Upton Park

Samuela Oppong (10)   166

St Joseph's Catholic Primary School, Redhill

Kezia Celestino (11)   168
Aizah Nadeem (10)   170
Khadija Asif (10)   172
Katie Mantke (10)   174
Chikuzierem Chime (10)   176
Max Brown (11)   178
Sebastian Watson (9)   180
Sara Oliveira (10)   182
Maria Joby (10)   184
Grace Edland (11)   186
Avaanesh Arruran (11)   188
Raphael Adetunji (11)   190
Leonardo Santin (10)   192
Narayah Andrews-Green (9)   194
Polina Maeyr (10)   196
Lily-May Wicker (10)   198
Natalia Rusilowska (11)   200
Nyla Funge (11)   202
Jamie Pettitt (9)   204
Alfie Pettit   206

St Julian's Church School, Wellow

Alfred Ward (9)   207
Harrison Lord (9)   208

St Malachy's Primary School, Belfast

Jood Ahmed (8)   209

St Mary's Catholic Primary School, Loughborough

Kazi Ullah (11)	210

St Mary's Hampton CE Primary School, Hampton

Sammy Dalby (9)	212

St Mary's RC Primary School, Edinburgh

Oliver Davidson (9)	213
Giorgia Pratico (10)	214

St Paul's CE Primary School, Leamington Spa

May Reynolds (9)	215

St Sebastian's RC Primary School, Douglas Green

Summer Taylor (10)	217
Davia Okon (10)	218

St Thomas More Catholic Primary School, Cheltenham

Lilly Edwards (10)	219
Kenzie Morris-Harker (10)	220

St Thomas' Primary School, Riddrie

Amelia Browarna (8)	221
Matteo Del Rossi (8)	222
Millie Ward (9)	223
Aaron Murray (9)	224
Olly Smith (9)	225

Stanley Crook Primary School, Stanley

Maisie Walker (11)	226

Strandtown Primary School, Belfast

Nathan Todd (8)	227
Ashlin Vijeesh (8)	228
Norah Armstrong (8)	229

Sybourn Primary School, Waltham Forest

Hajra Khan (8)	230
Izzabelle Madden (9)	231
Ashar Syed	232

Tarland Primary School, Tarland

Freya Wallace (8)	233
Amber Pittendreigh (7)	234

The Wilmslow Academy, Cheshire

Sam Holland (10)	235

Thompson Primary School, Thompson

James Sparkes (9)	236

West Linton Primary School, West Linton

Euan Brown (9)	237

Westonbirt School, Tetbury

Theodore Hickling (10)	238
Isabel Nassif (10)	240

Whitchurch CE Junior School, Whitchurch

Ryan Dodd (10)	241

Whitleigh Community Primary School, Whitleigh

Neve Powell (10)	242

Windlesham School & Nursery, Brighton

Lucia Sulley-Valent (10)	244
James Wadsworth (10)	245
Hermione Hawley (10)	246

Winscombe Primary School, Winscombe

Archie Brown (9)	247

Woodlands School, Great Warley

Elijah Ajala (10)	248
Teddy Spurling (10)	250
Toby Ajala (8)	251

Woodsetts Primary School, Woodsetts

Brooke Tomlinson (9)	252
Oliver Goodbold (9)	254
Poppy Dane (10)	255

Ysgol Bro Gwydir, Llanrwst

Millie May Jones (10)	256
Nel Roberts (10)	257
Jodi Jones (10)	258
Eban Jon Dafidd Roberts (10)	259
Phoebe Parry Owen (10)	260
Efa Jones (10)	261
Lela Mair Williams (9)	262

The Diaries

The Incredible Diary Of The Mysteries Of The Past

Dear Diary,

Unbelievably I have discovered the most unexplainable things ever. I found the most unexplained picture of the olden days and people wearing ancient clothes. Then, surprisingly, one person was wearing... modern clothes! I can't believe it. It's crazy.

The other day I came across a window and I saw an old-fashioned person riding a motorcycle and one second it was there and the next it wasn't! Some tried to explain this but we all just stood there with our mouths open, speechless.

I think some people have discovered time travel but keep it to themselves. Some people try and tell but no one will believe them. I would if I had the power. I would go to the scientists and ask them to show me. I'd travel at breakfast and then come back to the present!

Daisy Shapland (9)

Abbey Gates Primary School, Ravenshead

The Incredible Diary Of The Mushroom Kingdom

Dear Diary,

I have had what started as the worst day but turned into the best day! I went to school and did maths all day, it was very easy. Then I went back home but nobody answered the door so I just went in.

There was a piece of paper. It said that they had gone to the forest so that's where I headed.

I was looking for them for hours and hours upon hours and more hours until eventually, I found them. Right next to them was a beautiful mushroom kingdom.

Inside, it was a beautiful red and white floor and colourful red walls and a red rooftop. There were loads of mushrooms in there. One of the mushrooms said, "You need to transform into a mushroom." So that's what happened. My parents had run away because they didn't want to transform into a mushroom. I hope to see them again soon.

Stanley Weatherley (8)

Abermorddu Community Primary School, Abermorddu

Finding Nemo

Dear Diary,

Today when my family and I were swimming in the ocean, I went too far and deep then I got lost. When I got lost I was scared and nervous because I'm the youngest in my family. I'm a medium-sized clown fish with orange and white stripes. I have a brother called Dory, he is a lot bigger. Dory is blue and black. I was trying to look everywhere for my big friend Dory. I was now getting very worried because I was getting hungry and it was late. I wanted to find my family and I missed them so much. While I was in the ocean I was hunting for crab legs. I eat crab legs every day. My family and I like trying to go to the beach every day. After looking everywhere for my family I found them. I'm so happy!

Mya Gracie (9)
Alexander Peden Primary School And Nursery, Harthill

The Incredible Diary Of...

Dear Diary,

Today I had fun under the sea. I was playing with my orange friend. I was so happy and excited. We played and played until I had to go home.

When I was home I had seaweed and crab legs then I went for one last swim. I swam with my tiny fins but then my orange friend's dad said, "Your friend has been sucked up by a cylinder tube." I was so angry and sad but I had to save my friend so I found the cylinder tube and it sucked me up. Then I saw my friend but I realised I was in a fish tank as well. I took my orange friend and went up the tube.

Laci Worrall (10)

Alexander Peden Primary School And Nursery, Harthill

Spider-Man Stops The Train

Dear Diary,

Today I was on a roof on a tower in New York City and saw a train really fast. I made lots of webs to the train very fast. I tried and stopped the train from falling. I shot lots of webs to stop the train with my webs and slowed it down. I slowed it down by myself and I didn't need help with the train. Then I fainted and people caught me and took me to the train and a kid gave me my mask back. I went home and got my dinner and went to bed and got some sleep.

Declan Cleland (10)

Alexander Peden Primary School And Nursery, Harthill

Locked In A Tower

Dear Diary,

I've been locked in the tower since my mum went out. I'm in a tower with my little friend Camilion. Every day I stay in the tower while my mum goes out. When she comes back I let down my hair and she comes in. Sometimes my mum makes me sing a song and that makes my hair shine. My dream is to see the shiny lights that shine on my birthday. My mum says no though as she's afraid I will get hurt.

Naomi Mutukwa (11)

Alexander Peden Primary School And Nursery, Harthill

Black And White

Dear Diary,
I think I am an evil woman. I have a lot of dogs. I have half and half frizzy black and white hair. I wear vibrant red lipstick. I have a fabulous coat. I am also a really evil woman! I have a daughter. She is really evil too. And my coat is made out of special fluffy products. I have a movie that is the best of them all. I have big black boots that are nearly at my knees.

Charlie McNee (10)
Alexander Peden Primary School And Nursery, Harthill

The Racecar

Dear Diary,

I have a very famous profession. I am a racecar that is red, fast rookie. I raced through a giant crash today that made me fly. I am famous for my thunder and lightning. I am arch-enemies with Jackson Storm who is new and electric and fast.

Jeronimo Lynch (9)

Alexander Peden Primary School And Nursery, Harthill

A Day In The Life Of Mario

Dear Diary,

Today Bowser had been up to no good. I went under the sewers. We took Princess Peach to safety. We had a party with me, Luigi, Princess Peach, DK and Toad. We all had a fun time.

Nico Jaden Davidson (9)

Alexander Peden Primary School And Nursery, Harthill

The Incredible Diary Of The Little Mermaid

Dear Diary,

This morning I was minding my own business and I went to my mermaid bank and all my jewellery disappeared. I felt very, very sad so I told the merman owner. He was acting suspicious so I thought it was him. I said, "Give me my jewellery back now, thief."

Then he ran fast. I followed him from behind. We ended up at my favourite beach, where he had tried burying it in the soft sand. I discreetly dug it all out and became a super mermaid once again.

Janaat (9)

All Saints Junior School, Maidenhead

The Swimming Pool Trip

Dear Diary,

A couple of months ago I went to a swimming pool with my cousins. We went on a slide, we had pizza and ice cream and we had chairs to relax in. We also went to the deep end and we got Slushies inside the pool. There were seats to sit down on and there was a loopy slide. I went on the slide - it was very slow. After, we went back to my Albanian cousins and played with their Chihuahua. We had a fantastic time.

Joseph Kunora (8)
All Saints' CE Primary School N20, London

Symmetric-Al

Dear Diary,

I am halfway between my dangerous mission. I (along with four other close friends) have been chosen to defeat the legend of Symmetric-Al. We need to defeat him because he wants to destroy everything symmetrical so he can be the only symmetrical thing in the universe! So that means that we have to get a move on. I am not writing any more as I am on a boat at the sea of Wingardium and the waves are so big that I can't even relax!

Night.

Henry Halili (8)

Andrews Lane Primary School, Waltham Cross

The Boneless Man Who Lived In France

Dear Diary,

Instead of bones, he had breadsticks. The reason why he had breadsticks instead of bones was that when he was playing football in the park he fell over and it was raining so his hands got wet. After he had played football he went on the monkey bars and slipped off and he was on the floor with broken bones and had tears coming out of his eyes. He felt sad and hurt, but the good thing was that he could take a bite out of his arm, leg or spine when he was hungry. Mr Boneless Man is never going to the park in his life ever again.

Sully Spencer (8)
Bamford Primary School, Bamford

Dusty's Diary

Dear Diary,

Meow, meow, meow. Today I was strolling along when I saw another cat, it was licking its paws in the garden, my garden. Then I suddenly shot at it because it was in my territory and started fighting. After that, I went to the bottom of the garden and I saw a bird. I stared at it for a long time and then I jumped and caught it and I had bird pie for lunch. Meow.

Aidan Gower (8)
Bamford Primary School, Bamford

Nature's Sacrifice

Dear Diary,

I am sick and tired of silly people treating me like an uncivilised animal. The malady is that I provide them with an endless list of materials by commencing insipid errands; the least they could do is not inflict harm on me. It's only me that gets my torso chopped off and my legs left to rot. Anyway, they do it for the cattle, and soon kill them. The misery the childish fools weigh on my shoulders is undermining. Fortunately, fervent attempts to wipe me out are contradicted by the most sagacious mankind. How could they confront an innocent soul?! It is an unacceptable act that should be considered with severe consequences, yet the government continues to coax them to do it even more. Cruelty comes from their dead heart infected by anger and hatred, causing my tribulation era. What will happen when I am lost to the stars? Their time will cease to an end! Their hatred is endless and wrath is impactful.

No matter how painful this is, I cannot unleash my anger upon these beings. It would be unbearable to watch the harm unfolding before my own two emerald eyes.

"*Ouch!*" So sorry. That axe is really getting on my nerves and it's extremely painful. "Oh. That hurts, young man!"
There it is again. When will it ever end...?

Veer Khanna (9)
Bickley Park School, Bickley

The Gigantic Orange

Dear Diary,

Today, as I picked my freshly grown oranges, I came across a huge one. I couldn't believe it, I'd never seen anything like it! It was insanely hard to cut off the stem, but eventually I cut it off and the orange was rolling around the farm. It crushed all the fruit and veggies and squished into the yucky wet mud. The orange pushed the gate wide open, rolling into town, crushing the houses, shops, even skyscrapers. Everyone was screaming and shouting and I was running, trying to catch it. The town was ruined, no one could fix it. The orange was rolling around, it finally came to a stop at a large mountain. I was running for at least an hour. What am I going to do with it?

Jamie Everitt (10)
Brooklands Farm Primary School, Milton Keynes

Far From Home

Dear Diary,
I was far from home, I had nothing to do, I was in an abandoned shed and I was worrying if I was going to survive or die. I was thinking about the bad stuff that could happen tonight. There were just trees and an abandoned house but I was scared to go inside. My mother would say not to but I was going to go in the house for food... Inside the house was nothing but water and some food. I was craving crisps, meat and juice but I sadly found none of these things.

Abdullah Tahir (10)
Brooklands Farm Primary School, Milton Keynes

Hallie And Kiana

Dear Diary,

Kiana is the best friend I have ever had because I have done everything with her. I went into her pool with her and had tea. We did each other's make-up, went to the school park, went to the big park, had sleepovers and always play with each other in school. I have loads of other friends like Layla. She climbs trees with me and Kelsey, and that makes me laugh loads. With Maja, we went in a hot tub, on a slipping slide, had a sleepover in a tent, had tea and got a pizza. I have more friends but I'm telling you about my family.

Scott is seven years old. He has brown hair. Macie is twelve, turning thirteen. She has ginger hair. Evie has blonde and red hair. My dad has brown hair. Brooke has brown hair. She is fourteen years old. My mum has black hair. My nana has blonde hair and she got a new knee because she hurt her knee. My papa is lazy, all he does is sit on the chairs all day and tell me to come up with stuff he needs because his back hurts. I would rather go in my dad's car because he is faster than my papa.

Hallie Milligan (9)
Burnfoot Community School, Hawick

The Time I Saw The Amazing Taylor Swift

Dear Diary,

Today I had the time of my life. But let's start from the beginning.

I woke up. I was so excited because today I was going to see Taylor Swift. After a few minutes, we were in the car already and a few more minutes we were at the train station. It was really loud and crowded. We were finally on the train, there was lots to see outside, like sheep, horses and alpacas. After we got off the train everything was beautiful. For a second I thought I was in Dreamland!

It was a long walk but we were finally there. I was so happy because I was there with my sister and secondly, we had front-row seats.

Finally, Taylor Swift was on the stage.

Two hours later, my favourite song was finally here. It is '22'. As soon as the song was nearly finished I had to climb to get her hat and it was signed!

Autumn Bartlett (8)

Bushmead Primary School, Luton

Something Unexpected

Dear Diary,

Hi, my name is Lusy, I'm going to tell you about my weekend.

On Saturday morning, I was in bed, but then suddenly I heard footsteps coming up the stairs. It was Mum waking me up to tell me that breakfast was ready. You might be wondering why? Well, I always wake up last on weekends.

After that, I took my cat Teddy for a walk and did my morning run. I stopped at my friend Summer's house.

"Hi Lusy, nice to see you so early! Come in, Mum is making milkshakes!" exclaimed Summer with excitement.

We went towards the kitchen and everyone and everything disappeared. It was like we were dreaming...

Nimrah Ibrahim (7)
Bushmead Primary School, Luton

The Most Sensational Goal

Dear Diary,

It was a match between Manchester City and Inter. I was on the pitch, playing with my friends until full-time. I waited for my friend to pass to me and I lunged for acceleration and I passed all of the players. I was one-on-one with the goalkeeper. I stood back and I shot, but it crashed on the crossbar and went down over the line and it came back to me without hitting the net.

I asked the referee if that was a goal and it said that it was. 1-0. I screamed and ran to celebrate in front of my fans.

Suddenly I saw the referee blowing the whistle. I told everyone that we were now champions and we ran to lift the trophy. I screamed and screamed.

Shajidul Bhuiyan (11)

Buttercup Primary School, Whitechapel

The Fun Teacher

Dear Diary,

I had a fun day. I am a teacher and I told my students about everything I knew when I was a kid. I played football with my students and told them the rules of football. I put up a poster to tell people to help me and each day I would give a £10 note to them if they helped me teach my students.

One day a man called Hamaza saw the poster. He was a football teacher and he and I were friends. When he got the job my students really liked him, so much that we played football together. I asked my students if he should stay and teach them. He scored one million goals. He was unstoppable. The students started to get good at football.

Anzar Imtiyaaz (7)

Buttercup Primary School, Whitechapel

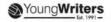

What A Watering Day

Dear Diary,

I went to the park with my brother and sister. I got the water gun from home. I was playing with another child. I got soaked a lot of times until my water gun ran out so I ran to my sister and she helped me fill up my water gun.

When I was tired I decided to draw on the floor with my water gun. The child that was playing with me found a lighter. I saw a family friend and when he saw the lighter he screamed and ran with his sister. I laughed when I saw my family friend screaming.

Then I got bored and I realised my sister went home. My brother said it was time to go home and he bought me a lollipop.

Aisha Ahmed (9)

Buttercup Primary School, Whitechapel

What A Lovely Day

Dear Diary,

I woke up early in the morning and wore my abaya and hijab, and my mum gave me my breakfast. I went to school and Miss Shaheda was starting next to the board and said, "As-salaam-alaikum, come in."

I said, "Wa-alaikum-assalam," and went in. I got my badge but I couldn't find it. I saw Uslad saying, "As-salaam-alaikum."

I said, "Wa-alaikum-assalam." I sat down and Miss Sultana came in. We went upstairs and down to maths. Miss Sultana said we would go to the park and eat ice lollies!

Jannate Ouaki E Alaoui (8)

Buttercup Primary School, Whitechapel

Cristiano Ronaldo In Al-Nasr

Dear Diary,
Today I joined Al-Nasr. I was overjoyed. I got 200,000,000 Euros. It was a lot of money! I left Juventus to go to Al-Nasr. My best match was Al-Nasr vs Paris Saint Germain. Me, Messi, Neymar and Mbappé. We won 4-3. They were on fire but so were we!
Bye, my name is Cristiano Ronaldo!

Abdurrahman Sewell (8)

Buttercup Primary School, Whitechapel

Best Day Of My Year

Dear Diary,

I went to an amazing zipline park and played on a humongous trampoline. Later on I went to my swimming lesson for two hours.

At night-time I thought that I'd had a more exhilarating day than ever before and my whole family had a great time.

Yusra Mohamed (9)

Buttercup Primary School, Whitechapel

My First Day At High School

Dear Diary,

I am Rachel, I've just left primary school. I will miss my teachers and friends. The first day of high school I saw my bestie, she ran over to me when we got there. The place was as big as an elephant. When I got to my locker I put my books inside. After that, it was time to go to the first-year presentation from the other class. Next, it was time for a break before classes before I went to the court where I found the cheese that was to be avoided because it had 'the cheese touch'. When I got to class I felt worried that I was going to embarrass myself.

Meanwhile, I was talking to my friends. I was at the door, I was starting to feel stressed. When I opened the door, eyes were staring at me. At that moment I saw a glowing stone. I picked it up and felt confused. I walked in and felt confident. After, I finished my classes and lunch.

It was a long day, but it was time to go home, sleep, do my homework, and explore the stone.

LaToya Micheal (9)
Cadder Primary School, Glasgow

A Little Painting - A Little Madness

Dear Diary,

I saw a young painter, about twenty years or more. In front was a beautiful painting, but she put her paintbrush down and sighed, "I won't finish this in time, nor will it be good enough for my art school portfolio."

I jumped out and said, "Hello, I see you're giving up. The painting never looks perfect as soon as you start." This happened in Canada.

She spat, "It needs to be perfect, it's for my art school!"

I felt a bit surprised. I said, "I think the real problem is how high your standards are. The painting looks great." She smiled and I zipped home.

Pearl Lin (9)

Cadder Primary School, Glasgow

Ant Invasion

Dear Diary,

It was madness... The fire ants and the black crazy ants were ruining our nest. Our tree (nest) was huge! We loved our tree but after the invasion, it was all just madness. I had no choice so I ran into battle but we, the carpenter colony, were unprepared and the fire and black crazy ants charged at us. Right at that moment another carpenter ant colony joined us to fight the other ant colonies. It was madness. Ants got killed and trampled over like little leaves. Soon we were winning! We had more troops and the fire and black crazy ants had no chance against us and we could finally take back the birch tree.

Terrence Gao (10)

Cadder Primary School, Glasgow

The Dress

Dear Diary,

This weird girl is always wearing me. I don't know why but let's find out... It all happened when she bought me for her birthday. Her dirty hands smelled like dog poo. They were so dirty that they stained me so I had to go in the washing machine. That was terrible. When I got out she hung me up. Now that felt great! Then she wore me for her birthday. When we went to Disney World I was so shy because people were looking at me. When I looked at myself I noticed that I was a sparkly rainbow dress. Now I understand and I feel very pretty.

Precious Izogie (9)
Cadder Primary School, Glasgow

Life Sucks

Dear Diary,

I am in so much pain. I get kicked every day. Everyone wants me. I am colourful, after all. I am covered in bruises. My life is so hard. It's the summer holiday, yay! You would think it's the best holiday but it's the worst! There is so much dog poo everywhere! You know, I hate my life but when it's winter it is cold and no one goes out except for the footballers. I went to the biggest football match and I got kicked so hard... Then I woke up and was shocked and I shouted out with fear.

Shay Mclaren (10)
Cadder Primary School, Glasgow

Paddington Bear

My name is Paddington. I am a bear from Peru. When I was little, I was going on a walk in the deep jungle with my aunt and uncle. There was a storm and the wind hit my uncle. He was hanging onto the bridge. Then the wind got worse and my auntie fell too and they sadly died. I was very sad because I had no family. I eventually came to a place called London. A nice and kind family found me in the streets and gave me a place to live. Goodbye for now.

Ava Kelly (10)
Cadder Primary School, Glasgow

A Day In My Life

Dear Diary,

I hate this, my body is hurting so bad because these people keep turning me on and off with their smelly fingers. When I don't have any more charge they don't care about me. I am so sad and they put spray on my face, I don't like it. All of my friends are on vacation because they're not used anymore but I am hot and I am tired of watching YouTube all day long.

Valeria Gamboa (10)

Cadder Primary School, Glasgow

Winnie And Friends

Dear Diary,

Today me and my friends went to go get something to eat. I had honey, Tigger had cake and Piglet had pink cotton candy. Then we went to the park. I went on the swing, the slide and the monkey bars. Then I came home.

Harper Omnet (9)

Cadder Primary School, Glasgow

The Incredible Diary Of A Spider

Dear Diary,
Today has been a hard day. I have been carrying over one thousand eggs on my back. I wish they would get off me because my back hurts so, so, so much. When they will hatch into small white spiders, I will get ready. So, I will go to get some bugs for my kids to eat. I better do it now because they're going to hatch soon. I know that because I can feel them kicking me through the eggs. I am going to hatch then. I should also make a bigger house for my kids somewhere else, I will have a nap right after all of that hard work.
My kids should be grateful for all of that hard work. I had to use all of my energy. If they are not grateful, I will kick them out of the house.
So, I am happy now because they hatched.

Simion Sauca (9)
Cannington CE Primary School, Cannington

The Incredible Diary Of Chavvy Lottie

Dear Diary,

I've had the worst day, ever! I hate school, everyone is so annoying, ew. So in the morning, I was doing my make-up of course, obvs late, I looked like a proper freak, and I was the same colour as a tangerine. My lashes looked like two flying butterflies when I was blinking. And if life could get any worse it was a Monday at school. I had already cried three times so I couldn't cry any more times. I put on my ugly uniform that made me gag. I could already feel it being a bad day. As I walked into the class I felt like everyone's eyes were on me. I walked to Isla (my best mate). I told her everything, she's the only person I don't hate. I asked her what was everyone's problem. She pulled out her iPhone 12 (she's rich and I'm jealous) and showed this ugly photo of me.

I did a disgusted face and I said, "What?" She then opened up Insta and I said, "No."

I understood what happened. Someone posted a picture of me. So everyone could see.

Izzy Pringle (11)
Chantry Middle School, Morpeth

The Incredible Diary Of Dylan

An extract

Dear Diary,

It's called the 'Medusa Project', the sin that caused all this chaos. I hate it, we hate it. By 'we' I mean me, Ketty, Nico and Ed. We all have psychic powers. I know what you're thinking Diary, *it's unreal! It's not possible!* Well, here we are. Four living psychopaths.

Wanna know our specialities? Ketty has the ability to tell the future, but she can't control it, just yet. Then there's Nico, he is the most powerful of us all, with telekinesis. He and Ketty are going out together (dating). Then there's also Ed, with the power to mind read and control people through their minds. Last but not least there's my lame... 'power' should I call it? But I only have the 'power' to protect myself from any danger I see coming. Yesterday we started our first mission. Oh, did I mention we have missions? Oh, never mind, it doesn't matter now. Anyway, we located the criminal easily, and then it was up to Nico to use his telekinesis to trap him, but it didn't work out and instead, the criminal pulled out a shotgun FA-K7. Nico tried to pry it from his warped fingers with his telekinesis but he gripped it too tight. There, here it comes, I was shot.

Blown off my feet, a cradle full of thoughts and emotions careered through me. Fear, embarrassment, pain. Yep! Mostly pain. Landing on the hard ground shred my shield to a million pieces. A bullet whizzed past my head, catching the tip of my ear as it did so. Since my shield was smashed I experienced more pain than ever. Warm hands gripped my arms and I felt the darkness seeping in...

Imogen Blewett (11)
Chantry Middle School, Morpeth

A Diary Of Unfortunate Events

An extract

Dear Diary,

Today I can say it was the worst day of my life as my sibling and I are very unfortunate but I will tell you what happened. A couple of days ago our parents died in a fire. It is a mystery how our home lit on fire but it did. We were in mourning when Mr Po came and informed me as I am the oldest. Since we are underage we needed to live with our closest living relative. We went to Count Olaf and immediately the first thing I noticed was his eye tattoo on his ankle. Anyway, back to earlier today, I heard last night he and his stage troop talking about a wedding for Count Olaf. I didn't think anything of it until I found out it was me getting married to him! I hated the idea so much as he only wanted to marry me because my parents left a colossal fortune for me to get when I am of age. What makes it even worse is that he is my legal guardian and with my legal guardian's consent I can get married underage because his next-door neighbour has many books so she had some about marriage and I read lots.

When I went back I said to Count Olaf, "I don't want to marry you."

He just said, "Okay!"

I didn't think it would go that well, because it didn't. I went to my room and in there was the dress. It was grotesque. I went outside to get some air and that's when I saw Sunny in a cage dangling from the roof. My jaw dropped.

Count Olaf approached me and said, "Marry me or say bye to Sunny..."

Annabella Huxley (11)
Chantry Middle School, Morpeth

The Incredible Diary Of A Star Pony

An extract

Dear Diary,

I am at a farm with my new rider Emily, who adores me (I mean who wouldn't?), the only thing is I am very cheeky which she says are 'my little blips'. *How rude! I am perfect!* For example, today we went for a ride down the lane. As I was getting tacked up I was *raring* to go until I accidentally lost my balance. I heard a crash, a scream from my rider and felt the saddle slide from my back.

"What's going on?" asked Logic - the mean and grumpy one of my *neigh*bours.

And a, "We're all going to die!" from my stupid, piebald friend Allegro.

Luckily, my saddle wasn't broken or damaged in any way so I could still strut my stuff. And that was only part of the mayhem I caused today. Five minutes into the ride, Allegro jolted to a halt but I carried on walking right into his bum. He started leaping around like a lunatic! I sped away as fast as I could, trying to get out of his kicking firing line while my rider was trying to calm me down.

Allegro finally finished when the booming voice of Bob shouted, "*Stop.*"

On the way home, Allegro and I both argued with the occasional complaint from Bob. We fought over cow parsley and tree leaves until my rider noticed what we were doing and yanked us away from the hedge. We reached home - no longer fighting - and were getting our blankets put on and Allegro was grooming the new foal (Coach) over the door.

Emily Havis (11)

Chantry Middle School, Morpeth

Gangsta Granny Returns: Ben's Diary Entry

Dear Diary,

Tonight has been crazy. It all started off by getting chased out of a dance competition by security guards. But when I went out onto the street I saw something come out of the pond by Buckingham Palace. I tried to be sneaky and I ran over the road and saw it was the Queen. She told me that she had been for a swim but I knew that was not true. So she sat me down and told me the story. She had taken both the World Cup and the mask of Tutankhamun. I couldn't believe it! The Queen had stolen them. But she wanted to return them. But we couldn't go dressed in a dance costume and a scuba outfit. So we headed to Raj's shop, surely he would have clothes. So we got our clothes but I was a princess. I didn't want to be that! But I got on with it. We headed to Wembley first but we got stopped by a policeman. Instead of talking with him, we tricked him into having a full shop of doughnuts (he fell for it). After that quickly headed off to Wembley. There was a quick obstacle with sprinklers but we got out just in time. Next, the museum.

We sped around corners and ears but luckily no one was hurt. We had to break locks and avoid some cameras (but it was like hide-and-seek). We quickly got out of there before the nosy neighbour caught up to us. We dropped Raj back off and I said goodbye to the Queen. I ran down the road as quickly as possible to get home. When I got home I saw a black cat so I knew it was a sign of a good night.

Grace Bell (12)
Chantry Middle School, Morpeth

The Incredible Diary Of Heather Oak

Dear Diary,

Today I got told to write a book about my life but of course it was boring English. I could not think of anything exciting. As time went by (to the end of the lesson) my page it was a polar bear in a snowstorm. Miss Black came around the class to check on our work. I got sent to Mr Brooks (aka the headteacher of doom). As soon as I had left I knew it was grounded but worst of all I didn't have an excuse for Mum. When the bus came to collect me, my sister (the best cover-up around) knew something was wrong.

"What have you done now, Heather?" said Holly in the nicest way.

When I got home you could hear the cats screeching, the car alarms going off and the worst, the monster steps (obviously Hannah Oaks, *my mom!*)."You will not hear the last of me," I told her. At the end of the crusade, guess what she had done. Grounded me and didn't let me get my Friday Fishy! I wish she understood what I have to go through, at least Holly does. That night I went to bed hungry. Wait, actually, I did have pizza and chips out of the freezer.

Oh, and Coco and Muffin were very good support cows. And Hannah Oaks better remember who she has messed with.

Charlotte Burn (11)

Chantry Middle School, Morpeth

The Incredible Diary Of Farmer Joe

Dear Diary,

Today was a fun day. Firstly I woke up which is always a horrid thing until I looked out the window and boom... The sun shattered my eyes as I fell backwards into my cosy bed. I hate the mornings but I always love it when I get to count my sheep. Ah yes, nearly makes me fall asleep. I was feeling extra enthusiastic so I put me old farmer's gear on and hopped in the tractor and off I rode to my good old sheep. I might shave them this year, the poor things.

Couple minutes later me and Betty arrived but something looked odd...

Counting sheep is so soothing until you realise you are missing three, which happened to me today. As I realised I was missing Trish, Pesh and Nesh, I hopped right back on the tractor and Betty and I went for a ride.

Couple minutes later I found one, it was Pesh. Excitedly I jumped out of the tractor and hopped on her. It felt like a cloud but we had to keep going. Over the hills and far away, I had found Nesh. Yes, excitement filled me up.

"Ah, who needs Trish?"
That's what I said before driving home.

Joshua Towers (11)
Chantry Middle School, Morpeth

The Disastrous Day Of Farmer Bill

Dear Diary,

Today I got up and had some toast and cereal then I headed out to work where I hopped into one of my many brand-new John Deere tractors and went to cultivate a field and it was going well so to get it done quicker I got one of my workers to help me. My tractor wouldn't start and I realised that it had emptied its oil on the ground and it cost me £200 to get it taken away. I then discovered one of my older tractors had been stolen. Listening to the weather forecast, there was going to be a *huge storm!* So I had to rush to get everything inside before this storm hit. I thought to myself, *why do these things happen to me?*

It was a new day and one of my sheds came down and put a two-by-four in the top of my tractor's roof. I got my stolen tractor back but the brakes were broken and it crashed into a tree.

Charlie Rutherford (11)

Chantry Middle School, Morpeth

The Story Of Super Long Nose

Dear Diary,

I am Super Long Nose but you're probably wondering why I am *called* Super Long Nose. I don't have a long nose but I had to pick a random name and it was the only one that came into my head.

Long story short, I am a Minotaur. I was going through a deep, dark, creepy wood and I saw a Minotaur and it came charging towards me. The next thing I remember, the smell of rotten flesh woke me, I glanced down to the sight of a hairy half-man and then suddenly saw a reflection of me with great big protruding horns on my head, I am half man I am half bull... *I am a Minotaur!*

I went home, my parents started screaming. I went to the hospital to get the Minotaur taken apart from me. So then we went home and had a happy but shaken dinner.

Mason Blight (11)
Chantry Middle School, Morpeth

World War One

Dear Diary,
1972, 2nd March. The war was here, bombs spread like wildfire. At the time I was only four years old, nearly my fifth birthday. Tears flowed down my rose-red cheeks, I was scared and alone. All I could hear were bombs and planes. The war booms were going off, people were banging on the door and my heart raced. I was stunned in fear. Someone opened the door. I opened my mind and jumped out, everything was burnt to the ground. I heard gunshots. I ran for my life, bombs going off, my head pounding. I was shuddering into tears, my mind flaming through my fingertips and then I saw a woman.
She said, "Come stay with me."
I went with her to her miniature bunker and I was safe.
Written by Maria Martin.

Alexa Hedley (11)
Chantry Middle School, Morpeth

The Mis-Con-Shuffle Dog Edition

Dear Diary,

Today was quite the experience. Daddy Pig and I went to the park and rescued a dog. The dog was adorable. We took it to the park and cuddled him but Daddy Pig threw the ball a bit too hard and we lost our dog! We saw a criminal deer taking our dog, we had to chase him down. By we, I mean me, Daddy Pig is too fat. Eventually, we got our dog back. Two weeks later we realised it wasn't our dog! We both laughed and laughed.

Jude Danby (10)

Chantry Middle School, Morpeth

Diary Of Thea Morris

Dear Diary,
Yesterday at 8:30am my dad was on his way to drop me off at school so he could go to work. He arrived at my school and dropped me off. "See you after school. Thea, your stepmum will pick you up," he said to me before he left. I said bye. Rapidly, I sprinted to my friends, said hi and put my phone in the office. The bell rang. I started to feel lightheaded. Suddenly, everything turned black. I woke up. "Where am I?" I asked. No one answered. My head started pounding. I started again (breathing heavily). "Help! Help! What's going on?" I managed to splurt out. All I could see was black, black as a black hole to be exact. Sprinting footsteps came to my rescue.
"Thea, what do you see?" someone asked panicked. I tried to say something, but nothing came out.
An eternity later I woke up with my stepmum and dad beside me. "Where is Mum? Where am I?" I asked, confused.
A guilty look spread across my dad's face. "She-she-she has gone missing," he replied sadly.

"What?" I exclaimed. "When. Who. Where. What?"
"She went missing yesterday while you were at school. Someone took her at the supermarket," my dad mentioned.
I couldn't stop the tears from rolling. I went back into a black hole. "Doctor! Doctor!" my stepmum screeched.
A random voice said, "She has a condition, there is no cure. I'm sorry, she will wake up in two minutes. Try to keep her calm."
That's how I found out about my condition.

Emily Ions (10)
Christ The King Catholic Primary School, Stockton-On-Tees

If I Were A Fish

Dear Diary,
If I were a fish I would like to be a shark.
I would eat other small fish. I would enjoy swimming in the ocean. I would be the fastest fish to swim. My skin would be very smooth. I would have big and long fins. I would swim until I reached other oceans and seas in other countries. I would stay in deep ocean waters where the whole world's mysteries exist.
I would have very good company. I would interact a lot with fish of my size and shape. On the way, I'd pass through many fish colonies and interact with all kinds of fish. I would be good friends with other sea creatures. I would enjoy my freedom in abundance. And I would try my best not to eat any sea divers.

Muhammad Mustafaul Haque (8)
Claycots School, Slough

My Family And Friends

Dear Diary,

I love my friends and family. They treat me well and they help me. Well, my friends are nice to me and my family are sweet to me, that is why I love them very much.

On Father's Day, it was a special day for my dad. That day we went to Creams and had so many treats and they were delicious.

My friends are also nice because every time they come to me when I am emotional and they are also kind and respectful.

I also want to talk about my nice and kind teacher which is Miss Beeley. She is a calm person and every time is nice to me. I love my teacher as well.

Maryam Babne (9)
Claycots School, Slough

A Day In The Life Of Poppy

Dear Diary,

Today I had the best day ever! Besides these things. So it all started when... Wait, I need the loo, I'll be right back.

Five minutes later...

So now I will tell you. So first I smelled something horrible, so I shouted, "Sarah, was that you?" No answer, I tried again. "Sarah, was it you?" Still no answer. "*Sarah!*"

She finally answered.

"*Yes?*" she screamed.

"Did you do it?" I said.

"*Eww!* No! Never ever!" she responded.

"If it wasn't me, nor you, who was it?" I said back.

"Fluffy..." we whispered.

A guilty look appeared on her face.

"Was it you?"

Of course, she didn't say anything but a meow, but it was a suspicious meow, a strangely weird-sounding meow. So we called it a yes, a proud yes.

Then after all that I tripped over a person's foot and that person was...
"Girls, come down for tea!"

Olivia Wood Rose (10)

Comely Park Primary School, Falkirk

Adam's Day At A New School

Dear Diary,

Today me and my friend, Max, went to a new school called Coteford Juniors. On the way, I saw Max. He said hi to me and I said hi back. I showed him my rare Pokémon card. I said, "Do you know it's rare?"

He said, "Wow!"

Then we were at school and it was big so I walked in. The people were nice to me. Miss Bowerman was the best teacher but people were talking during class and we were doing maths clockwise and anticlockwise. It was hard but I learned something. Next was playtime. I lined up like the others. I played with Max and we were racing around but then we went in and did English. Then it was lunchtime. I had school dinners. It was nice then we did PE. We did cricket. It was fun then we went home.

Millie-Mae Lupton (9)
Coteford Junior School, Eastcote

The Incredible Diary Of A Shooting Star

Dear Diary,

Yesterday, I travelled to the supernova. It was beautiful. Also, I floated everywhere. I floated everywhere but I flew even higher. Then I was a bit afraid and anxious. It all happened in the wonderful, beautiful Thailand. I was a bit nervous. Afterwards, I was as confused as a child that doesn't know maths. Also, I looked a bit nervous. I got blue because I got hit by the super solar bands and the iconic solar system. Also, my head hurt so badly.

See you soon, Diary.

From Shooting Star.

Aathira Sutharsan (8)

Cowley St Laurence CE Primary School, Cowley

The Incredible Diary Of A Unicorn

Dear Diary,
I woke up yesterday and went to the magical market and then after that I went to the shopping mall. I took some make-up things and then I went home and watched TV. I was eating popcorn then I had a good sleep.

Nidha Ann Saju (8)
Cowley St Laurence CE Primary School, Cowley

The Cool Dad

Dear Diary,

My dad was a racecar driver and one day he had a bad crash. He had two broken bones, a leg and an arm. He was in a wheelchair for six months. He made a hard decision, he quit.

I was heartbroken but my dad got me everything and he worked for bad people. One week later he was working at a business and we live a happy life.

Ewan Fraser (10)

Cradlehall Primary School, Westhill

The School Drama

Dear Diary,

It was a Thursday and I was in school. We were listening to music while doing maths and I got a note handed to me. The boy who handed it to me was Jake the popular boy. He said it was from Angela. I knew that wasn't good.

While I was opening it I was shaking and my hands were sweating. I opened it and it said 'Meet me at the rooftop at 1:15'. I binned the note. I glanced over to Angela. She had an evil smile on her face that made me feel threatened and a bit frustrated with myself. I needed to toughen up a little.

I continued to finish off my maths. The bell rang very soon and I had to go to the rooftop. As soon as I got there she cornered me. She whispered, "Your life is going to go downhill."

I ran off before she could say more. She was very mad but I didn't care. I stopped to breathe for a few minutes.

I was fed up. I asked my brother to help me, he said yes. I told him the plan and he agreed. The plan was for tomorrow. I would act like I didn't care and if she hurt me I would get my brother to defend me. So I ignored her. She shouted and screamed. She was mad, very mad.

The next day she punched me in the face and my brother came and calmed both of us down and told her, "Violence is not key, just talk about it." After that we became friends.

Kourtney Mackenzie (9)

Cradlehall Primary School, Westhill

The Incredible Diary Of Rocco And Tim The Monkey

Dear Diary,

I was in my bed watching videos. I was off school. I was ready to go and explore the trees I was checking out yesterday near the grammar school. Oh, of course, I can't forget Tim the Monkey.

We got there after a five-minute walk. We decided to go to the wee forest and saw the griffin again. For those who don't know what a griffin is, it's a lion mixed with an eagle. It was sleeping this time. It was guarding something. It wasn't babies, it was something else. I felt brave so I decided to go and see what it was.

While I was walking I stepped on something and it made a cracking sound. Oh no! I woke up the giant beast. Tim jumped off my shoulder. "No, Tim! Come back!"

I got home and tried to find a magnifying glass. I looked in the bottom drawer and found one.

I went back to the spot where Tim ran away. I started to look for footprints with my magnifying glass. I found a couple of them but I couldn't find more than five. I decided to go and scare the griffin.

I saw the beast and I saw Tim on the griffin's back. I had to save him. "Tim! Run!"

Tim ran back onto my shoulder and we slayed the beast. We told it to leave Tim alone. We ran back home.

Rocco Freeman (9)

D H Christie Memorial Primary School, Coleraine

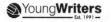

A Day In The Life Of Mike Tyson

Dear Diary,

I am Mike Tyson. I am a famous boxer. I have quite a lot of knockouts. I have forty-four knockouts. I have had fifty-eight fights, fifty wins, forty-four wins by KO and six losses.

One particular day I was feeding my pigeons when there was a group of boys. They came up to me and asked me if they could hold my bird. When he was holding my pet bird, it was chirping too much and he ripped its head off.

I was in a boxing ring and they put me up against someone way too old and good for me. He was beating me. I caught him with an uppercut and knocked him out.

Danny Doherty (9)
D H Christie Memorial Primary School, Coleraine

The Weirdest Day Ever

Dear Diary,

Yesterday was the most interesting day. I started a new school, I was so excited but then I got bullied. When I was back at the house I got ready for bed after playing with my friend Isla. She had come over to my house for a sleepover. When me and Isla went to my room, Isla's dog, Bruno, was in my room and I found out he could talk. Isla said, "Jess, I need to tell you something. My dog has multiple powers like talking!" I found this really weird and wondered why he was in my house.

I told her I was getting bullied and she said not to worry, she told Bruno and he thought he could help. He said, "We have to swap bodies!"

Today he went to school as me and Bruno talked and made friends with the bully and now I won't have any more problems at school and will be very popular!

Isla Ferguson (9)

Eastern Green Junior School, Coventry

The Chaos Of Number 5

Dear Diary,

Today I was being used like crazy. First I was in Year 3 and then in Year 2. Then Year 3 and then in Year 4. I am number 5, my name is Flo Foblo. I am the only number with a name because 6's name is 6 and I hate being the number 5. I never get a rest like 6666669, who always gets a rest. Today I had an idea, I should move next to 2222250. I will then get a rest but I will miss number 4 and number 6. I will only be in Year 1 tomorrow so school will be nice and quiet at West Blue High School. I will be sad though if I move but will be happy to get a rest. I don't know what to do. Please help!

From Flo Foblo.

Bailey Dalton (8)

Eastern Green Junior School, Coventry

The Footballer's Best Day

Dear Diary,

Today I was going to a football match. It was going to be a tough match. When I went outside the crowd was going mad and I started from the other end of the pitch. I was playing against PSG, my arch-enemy! As the children followed behind us, we sang and then we were ready to play the game. The game started and PSG were pushing strong. Neymar tried to score and missed. I got the ball and scored with a bicycle kick. The crowd cheered and we scored two more goals. The match then ended which meant the game had finished. It was a good game.

Boaz Ibitoye (9)

Eastern Green Junior School, Coventry

Geography Nerd, Or Not!

Dear Diary,

I am Jack Suck At Life, also known as Jack Massey Welsh. I am just writing to say that every time I say geography I get worse at geography. Today I was just drawing the flags with their names but I couldn't even remember my favourite... the St Lucian flag. I got really sad as I have spent the last five years trying to learn geography. Wait, oh no, geography again, it's all too much! No!

Danny Turner (9)

Eastern Green Junior School, Coventry

Speed Got Lost

Dear Diary,

Today was the worst! I was going to the woods when I heard Speed's roar. I knew he was lost. I could soon see he was stuck in a tree. I zoomed to Speed but I was shocked, Speed was trying to get a baby dinosaur. In the end, everyone was safe and me and Speed decided to never leave each other's side. Speed, my best friend, well his mum invited me to lunch and we had a good time.

Georgia Gibbs (9)
Eastern Green Junior School, Coventry

Diary Of An Ice Lolly

Dear Diary,

Today had been a hectic day and a lot has happened. I was in a refreshingly cool white box and the next thing I knew, a giant pair of hands were lifting me out. I could still see the box that I'd come out of.

I got passed to another pair of hands, slightly warmer than the last pair. I was very scared and nervous because I didn't know what was going to happen to me. The person that I got passed to started to strip me naked! Then he passed me to his child who bit my head off and then started licking my body. In her stomach, my head and body were attached back together.

By the next day, I was in this other white tank, not as cold as the first white box that I was in yesterday. Anyway, when the child saw me she screamed and screamed for her mum. Eventually, after what felt like millions of miles, I found my way back to the white box I started in.

The strange thing was that this happened several times apart from once when I forgot to get out of the warmer white tank. Someone pressed a button and water went everywhere. I was being sucked down a series of pipes until I went to this massive pool of salty water.

Then I went through more pipes into a reservoir. Then I went through a series of pipes, pumps and filters. I then went into a tap and got mixed with water and Fanta to make a new ice lolly.
I hope tomorrow is as good as today. Bye!

Amelia Haywood (9)

Edgbaston High School For Girls, Edgbaston

The Incredible Diary Of Mary

Dear Diary,

It was finally here. It was my birthday. I leapt out of bed and raced down the stairs to what my parents had planned for me. Opening the door in excitement, there was nothing...

"Did you forget about my birthday?"

This is the worst birthday ever.

That afternoon, I caught my mum and dad doing something secret. I was confused but I didn't bother asking them.

When I went back downstairs, I couldn't believe my eyes. There was a little kitten purring at me. I have always wanted a cat as a pet. I changed my mind... this is the best birthday ever.

I don't think any day will be better than today.

Hitha Inamadugu (8)

Edgbaston High School For Girls, Edgbaston

The Diary Of Triclaw

Dear Diary,

My name is Triclaw and I am a shape-shifter. Everyone in my world is all born with a power, I never got to see my parents' power because they died before I was old enough to meet them. One day I was eating birds as a feisty alligator in the tropical Amazon rainforest. Suddenly a dinosaur came out of the sky and roared, "I am going to destroy this village!" I think his power was to travel through portals. Anyway, I tried to destroy him but accidentally flew through his portal. I could have tried to fly back but I couldn't leave his house as it was very luxurious, I wouldn't say the same about his food.

Haaniya Sabir (9)
Edgbaston High School For Girls, Edgbaston

The Incredible Diary Of Aditi

Dear Diary,

I was woken by the sound of my grandpa stomping up the stairs to wake me. I suddenly realised that it was my 10th birthday.

An hour after I got changed, we went to the airport to go to Italy. I was so excited and my mum told me that I could have a pizza every single day. After hours of waiting, we finally got the plane. We got there really quickly but then everyone suddenly realized that the plane had landed at the wrong airport. We were supposed to land at Milan airport.

Aditi Mohanraj (10)

Edgbaston High School For Girls, Edgbaston

The Cookie

Dear Diary,

I am in a person's stomach. I was a huge cookie but now I'm the size of an ant.

It happened at ten o'clock. I was in a party room. I knew what would happen. My friends were dying and I would soon be dead too. I forgot I could teleport but I suddenly remembered in my flashback. I teleported and I was free. I still got eaten but I'm okay. I'm slowly dying again. I'm bleeding chocolate. Sadly I'm going to die now. My life was okay...

Ariane Li (9)
Edgbaston High School For Girls, Edgbaston

Diary Of An Unexpected Day!

Dear Diary,

Today I found myself in a clamshell. I was nearly falling asleep when I saw a gleaming light as bright as the sun. There was a crowd cheering loudly. The crowd said that I had been stuck in the clamshell for ten years.

I was confused so I asked calmly where I was. They said I was in Wales. When I got out of the shell, I was so exhausted so now I'm in a luxurious hotel on my bed.

This was my day, I hope I don't get stuck in a clamshell again.

Ruth Li (8)

Edgbaston High School For Girls, Edgbaston

Getting Back To Hogwarts

Dear Diary,

Today I was at Uncle Vernon's and as you can imagine he got really mad so I could not wait to go back to Hogwarts. The summer holidays were almost over, I was so excited to see Ron and Hermione and to get my new school books but I think my house room will look the same. I was back on the train eating a chocolate frog when I saw Rob and Scabbers.

Effie Smalldridge (9)

Edward Worlledge Ormiston Academy, Great Yarmouth

The Mystery Of The Diary!

Dear Diary,

Today was terrible. My bully, Mckayla, took my diary and I still can't find it. That's why I'm writing on this paper. I am so annoyed. I am going to get Mckayla back. Luckily, I have my friends; Chloe and Lola, to help me.

As I was checking my locker, Chloe came up behind me and said, "Mckayla is in her locker. We can glue her to her locker with my stationary kit."

I thought Chloe was joking but she is now getting her stationary kit. Mckayla will kill me! And Chloe! Lola got out of this because she had a dentist appointment.

Mckayla finally gave me my diary back! Yay!

Kasia Snopek (8)

Emneth Academy, Emneth

Escape From Pompeii

August 24th, AD79

Dear Diary,

What a horrific day I've had! As the day progressed, I grew worried. Worry turned into distress. Distress turned into hate. I hated that stupid volcano!

First thing in the morning, I got cereal, got dressed and curled my hair. On my way to the cupboard, I saw my dad. At first, I felt uneasy. After the conversation, I went to find Tranio.

I went outside and saw Tranio waiting for me. We played knucklebones in the streets. His dad shouted for him.

In the afternoon, the ground started to shake. Suddenly, the clouds went grey like the strands in my hair. The ground stopped. It started raining but the ground repeated. As I was running, ash fell on my arm.

At that moment, I heard a bang. Then I felt really uneasy. I looked to my right and saw an erupting volcano. I hope Tranio and his dad are okay.

Kelsey-Leigh Greenhough (10)

Farfield Primary & Nursery School, Bradford

Escape From Pompeii

August 24th, AD79

Dear Diary,

What an uneasy day I've had! As the day progressed, I grew increasingly alarmed. Alarm turned into anger. Anger led to hate. I hate that betraying beast.

First thing in the morning, I looked out the window. Then, I felt uneasy because the birds were flying in the wrong direction. The cloudless sky made me feel a bit better yet I still had an uneasy feeling. After breakfast, I snuck to the port and watched them get wine jugs. Then, I went to the theatre to watch Father. As I was there, I heard people start to sing a silly song called 'Rumble Down, Tumble Down'. I then went to Livia's house to play knucklebones. It was so fun.

Suddenly, the ground started to rumble uncontrollably and the sky started to fill with ash. I thought it was a joke at first but I started to realise it wasn't a joke. Everyone was running, screaming and grabbing their belongings. Livia and I were small enough to go through.

We went to the port to escape and got in a boat. We then watched as everyone screamed because our great protector betrayed us. We then fell asleep on the boat. I wonder what happened to my family.

Friday 12th January, AD109
Dear Diary,
Last week, I went to my childhood town. It brought back so many memories. I should have never gone back. As I woke up the kids to get breakfast, I looked out the window like I did when I was younger.
I checked if the birds were flying the right way. That day when I looked out the window the birds were flying the wrong way. The day the volcano erupted everyone was screaming. I will never forget that day.

Lily Kelley (9)
Farfield Primary & Nursery School, Bradford

Escape From Pompeii

August 24th, AD79

Dear Diary,

What a menacing day I've had! As the day went by, I grew increasingly fearful. Fear turned into worry. Worry turned into fright. A frightening thing came along.

First thing in the morning, I looked out of the window and felt surrounded and engulfed in bad feelings. I shook it off and went to set the fire up for the bread. After setting everything up, I went out for Tranio.

After getting Tranio, we went to the theatre to watch his father teach the actors. The actors unexpectedly started to sing our favourite song called 'Rumble Down, Tumble Down'. Me, Tranio, his father and the actors were laughing after the song.

Eventually, we left and a few seconds later, the ground trembled. Ash and lava were spewing out of the furious betraying volcano. We ran and ran while the lava chased us. Me and Tranio started to choke so we covered our mouths.

Finally, we ran and hopped on a stranger's boat. We cried as we watched our home go down in lava-fueled flames. It was terrifying. The man took us to

Greece. I wonder if my friends and family were still alive.

23rd August, AD89
Dear Diary,
Yesterday, I went back to my childhood home with my two-year-old daughter and husband. I regret ever going back. The scattered memories haunted us for the rest of our life. Our daughter ran into the fixed playground we played in as kids.
Me and Tranio smiled and tried not to bring a horrified face to our daughter's happiness. My life will never be the same.

Ellie-Jo Cawley (9)
Farfield Primary & Nursery School, Bradford

Escape From Pompeii

August 24th, AD79

Dear Diary,

What a horrific day I've had! I grew increasingly anxious. Anxious to depressed. Depressed to hate. I hate Mount Vesuvius.

Immediately in the morning, I looked out the window but I had an uneasy feeling. I did not know why. The sea was a vivid, blue colour and the clouds were bright white but my head still had an uneasy feeling.

I ate breakfast and ran to the port to see the Greek fisherman getting all the fish to the boat. I took some fish to give to my father. I went back home. My father ran out and grabbed my hand. We ran but I was confused. We went to the theatre. He talked about his performance. It was good with the sword but I got bored and I sneaked out.

I saw smoke. I ran to Tranio and his dad ran to get the donkey. I laughed so hard everyone could hear it but I told him to run.

We tried to find a boat. We ran to go to the boat but I and Tranio saw lava spewing out of the mountain and we cried so hard. I felt as if my heart had broken into millions of pieces.

Friday 14th July, 119AD

Dear Diary,

One week ago, I went to my childhood home. It was the worst idea ever. I got a job and had children. Livia and I got married. We thought it would be a good idea to go back. I wish I never came back.

David Cenuse (9)

Farfield Primary & Nursery School, Bradford

Escape From Pompeii

Dear Diary,

What a fun day I've had!

I jumped out of my bed and stormed downstairs and got Lucky Charms. Suddenly, I heard a strange knock on our dusty door. Livia said, "Do you want to play more knucklebones?"

I said, "Okay, how many rounds of knucklebones do you want to play?"

"Two, is that alright?" replied Livia.

"We should do this more often."

"Yeah, I think we should," replied Livia.

"I hope in the future we can do more days like this."

"Come over again and we can play more knucklebones."

Two hours later...

"Should we go to the theatre?" said Livia.

"Sure!" I replied.

"What should we watch?

"The pantomime?"

"Oh, that sounds fantastic!" Livia said.

When the pantomime finished, we got out of the theatre and saw a volcano erupting violently. I was scared because the volcano was erupting. We got on a boat and fell asleep.

When we woke up, Livia looked at me and then ahead at the sight of terror in the distance. We were horrified. Pompeii was getting further away and we could barely see it any more as it was covered with black ash. What will tomorrow bring? Will anyone survive?

Kyen Whitaker (9)

Farfield Primary & Nursery School, Bradford

My Holiday

Dear Diary,

A few weeks ago it was the best day of my life. My mum, my sister, my mum's best friend, my friend and I went on a plane but I didn't know where it was going but on the way there my friend and I played some games and watched a movie. The train ride after was about five hours. When we got off my mum told me where I was, I was in Greece. We checked in at our hotel and went swimming in the hotel pool. After swimming we went to look around the ancient cities. After looking around it was 9pm so we went to our hotel. Tomorrow we will get the ferry and visit Turkey.

William Banning (10)

Fir Tree Primary School & Nursery, Newbury

My Baby Sister

Dear Diary,

My baby sister, her name is Zara, was born on the 11th of March. She was cute and cuddly. She is the best sister in the world and adorable. She is four months old now.

Ruby Draper (10)

Fir Tree Primary School & Nursery, Newbury

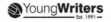

Cinderella

An extract

Dear Diary,

It's me, Cinderella. I'm so tired. I have to do all the chores, like cleaning the floor, washing the dishes, ironing the clothes, mopping the floors, vacuuming the house, tidying the beds, and brushing the carpet.

This morning, while I was cleaning the windows, I saw a letter on the floor. I picked it up and read it. It wasn't for me, it was for my stepmother. I gave it to her and told her the prince had arranged a ball for the finest people in the village. She sent me to iron the clothes, polish the shoes, and do their hair. Once I did all the jobs and my stepmother and stepsisters had gone to the ball, I ran into the living room and cried. As I was crying, a fairy popped out of nowhere and gave me a piece of paper. After, she vanished. I opened the piece of paper, it said to touch the wall.

I touched the wall, like it said. A beautiful ballgown was inside. I put it on. Then I heard a beep outside. I opened the door and saw a beautiful carriage. I hopped on. Then it teleported to the prince's castle. I was amazed to see so many people!

After that beautiful sight, I went inside. It was amazing. There were drinks, cakes, pastries, crisps, and sweets of all kinds, like fudge and caramel. Then I saw a watch. I had to be out of the castle before twelve o'clock!

Salma Khatun (8)
Grafton Primary School, Holloway

The Incredible Diary Of Pixi The Red Fox

An extract

Dear Diary,
It was Monday morning and today, in Fox Laws, you could hunt your own food! There I was, on my first day of being twelve. Mum was up, so I could ask for breakfast. Chicken and worms, my favourite!
First, I had to play with my sisters, Trixi and Mixi. We went into the fields, where we played. We love jumping into pillows of buttercups. But when I jumped, I realised I killed a rat. I felt so grown up! I took it back. That night, we had rat for dinner.

Dear Diary,
I woke up. Today was moving day! So I packed my bags. We were walking and OMG, this got cringe. There's this fox called Barry and he has a crush on me, but I don't. He came over and acted lovey-dovey. I rolled my eyes and I kicked him, then he went.
Luckily, one hour later, we were here. My legs ached. The den is much bigger. And best of all, my best friend, Heather, is our next-door neighbour. For the day, we sunbathed, me, Trixi, Mixi, and Heather.

Dear Diary,

It was one in the morning and I swore I could see something. It wasn't a squirrel, not a fox, but something alive... I was petrified, glued to the spot. It was a grass snake! It was coming toward me. I had a bit of fun. Want to know what I did? I just tied it into five knots and threw it out the door.

Amelie Malach (8)

Grafton Primary School, Holloway

Ruler's Diary

Dear Diary,

Ugh! I am fed up with everyone playing with me. I am supposed to be used to draw straight lines or measure something. I don't like people bending me! I do not feel like a ruler anymore because I am not straight.

The children in the classroom probably got in trouble because they were playing and bending me and the other rulers. Some of the children were putting rubbers on the rulers and then throwing the rubber in the air!

Then, all of a sudden, the headteacher came in and said, "What is all the noise for?" Then everybody went silent and he said again, "What is all this noise for?"

The teacher said they were playing with rulers and fighting. The headteacher said, "Why were you playing with rulers?"

One child said to the teacher, "Can I go to the toilet?"

The teacher was shocked! The person who asked to go to the toilet was the person who started playing with rulers and fighting! The teacher burst out the word no!

Safiyah Ahmed (8)

Grafton Primary School, Holloway

98

The Murder Date

Dear Diary,
You will never ever believe what happened yesterday. Well, I was walking back home from school when I saw Gerald, from class. And guess what? He had a crush on me! Well, I just acted, you know, all lovey-dovey.

He came to me and said, "Eh, I have been waiting for this moment. Will you go on a date with me?"
In my mind, I said, *Oh my gosh! What should I say? I don't wanna go, he can't even say 'date' properly! Oh my god, what should I say? I should probably say yes to be kind anyway.*

Sadly, I said okay. I regret it because we are going to a restaurant and he better be paying because I am not going to pay for anything he eats!

Dear Diary,
Oh well, you know what day it is. The dumb date. Ugh. So, I went. I dragged him to the toilet and... I killed him! I hope I don't go to jail! Eek!

Ceyda Kaygusuz (8)

Grafton Primary School, Holloway

Mani's Diary

Dear Diary,

Uh! Today was so exhausting! This morning, Chief told me Petey had escaped! For the ninth time! He also told me I had to catch him. I always have the hard job.

Anyway, I went after Petey but I saw something in his hand. It was a button. I ran faster and caught him and when I caught him, he pressed it. The next thing I knew, I was being shot by a robot!

I ran as fast as I could go, then I had an idea. I jumped on the back of the bot, chewed the wire, and took Petey to jail.

Niaz Miah (7)

Grafton Primary School, Holloway

Ronaldo

Dear Diary,

Today, I had a football lesson but it was cancelled so I went home and practised and practised. I went to the football pitch and played. My team got ten points! I was shocked and I went to tell my friend. I was happy for that.

But my son jump-scared me and my daughter and the baby. Suddenly, everyone was sad because their team lost. Everyone was on the pitch. The fans started shouting. I felt sorry for the fans.

Ridwan Ibrahim (8)

Grafton Primary School, Holloway

The Alien Chicken

Dear Diary,
There was a chicken coming out of a UFO and everyone was running. It looked like a troll and it flew off. I was in the playground, playing, until I saw it flying. I was on the swing and it bit me hard! It really hurt. I had to walk home. The next day, I saw it again and the UFO was back. It got the chicken. The UFO looked strange.

Jaylen Carrera (8)
Grafton Primary School, Holloway

Mr Big Brains And The Invention

Dear Diary,

Since last Saturday everybody has started to hate me. All because of my invention. I tried to make the world a better place, but it has turned into a disaster. I wanted a dinosaur as a pet but I didn't realise making that a reality would destroy my city. I invented the time machine so that humans could go back and use the resources that we've already used. While I was testing it out I found an extremely cute dinosaur. I decided to take him back home. And when I fed him he then grew 20 feet taller. He broke my roof and rushed into the city and started to break all the houses. Bricks flew through the air like aeroplanes.

And that's why everybody has started to hate me.

Gideon Adams (9)

Greenfield Primary School, Stourbridge

Diary Of A Japanese Cat

Dear Diary,

Today a disaster happened, so firstly my annoying sister started jumping on my precious, warm, fluffy bed. At 04:00. Um, sis, I think I scheduled my alarm for 12! It actually said 02:00, sorry. My mind auto-corrects itself. I think I say 4 in my mind way too much.

9:00

Well, I didn't wake up at 12. I woke up at 9. But that's only because my neighbour's cat, Emi, rang the doorbell and I had Yasuko, my dog sister barking at Emi. I suppose Emi ran away because when my annoying owner's daughter opened the door, nothing was there. Not even a dust of wind. However, I did see Tamako running past our gate, but that was it really. At 9:30 it was only really me. So you know what I did? I went to the local park. The eye-catching pulchritudinous Daisen-Oki Park. It's where I go for my daily stroll and it only takes about 15 minutes to get there.

10:05

When I got there, I climbed the Sakura cherry blossom tree. Get it? Because Sakura's my name? Wait, did I climb the right tree? This seems a lot higher.

Wow! I can see my irritating sister's school. But seriously I need help. Okay, this is just getting weird, I can see Hogwarts. What? How high am I? Hogwarts is like in Great Britain or something! Okay, I'll tell you a secret... I only have one life left and I am definitely not wasting it here. I won't waste it until I find something actually fun.

13:00

Someone finally called the firefighters and I'm falling. Wait, what is that? A trampoline? They use that? That was so fun! Oh my god!

21:00

That certainly wasn't what I expected but it was definitely worth it. I wanna do that every day.

Chloe Ainsworth (9)

Grosvenor Road Primary School, Swinton

The Life Of Twirl

Dear Diary,

Last week I was on my planet Cocoa. If you don't know I'm a chocolate bar that escaped from his planet. My name is Twirl. I didn't like my planet because everyone was mean and didn't listen to me so I travelled to Earth and landed in a shop called Chocolate City. It was spectacular there. Lots of people were buying chocolate, it felt so good to be loved. I felt very honoured. I was in a silver and gold container then I got bought and I lived a good life.

Mohammed Gabralla (9)

Grosvenor Road Primary School, Swinton

A Day In The Life Of Bella The Royal Cat

Dear Diary,

Today was a great day. This morning I mischievously decided to wake up Jazzy by licking her ear (she didn't like that!). Then she fed me my gourmet food (treats). Soon after that I hopped outside and fulfilled my royal duties which include standing on tables, breaking expensive things and being annoying! Then I jumped on my trusty steed Charlie (well Charlie isn't really a horse, he's a dog). Later that night I slid out the cat flap and went to see my good old friend Olly. He is my best, best friend. We had a secret meeting... I can't say anything about that. Whoops! So that was what I did today. Goodbye.

Jasmine Holmes (9)

Hartlebury CE Primary School, Hartlebury

The Midnight Crab

Dear Diary,

Hi, my name is Lacy! Two long days ago, this amazing story happened...

As I got home from school, everything was normal. I went in my room without seeing my parents. I thought they went shopping. It started getting really late, so I went out to search for my parents. I went in the forest without thinking.

I got to a place that looked sus. "Aah!" I screamed as I fell. I thought I knew where I was: the backrooms! I saw a sign that said: *Do This Obstacle* so I jumped and I ran. Then I saw a bunch of crabs. I went and started dancing and they started bouncing up and down. Then a monster came and danced with us.

Zoe Nyerges (9)
Highgate Primary Academy, Goldthorpe

New Friends

Dear Diary,

In 2019, my mum died. It was not the same without her. My happy feelings went down every day. Then, in 2021, I went to a school. Everyone moved out of my way and stared at me.

Then it was lunchtime. I was sat on my own and the same thing happened for four weeks until a girl came to me. Her name was Sam. We played for five weeks, then she said that she was using me. A boy came to me. His name was Oliver. On June 3rd, Sam set a fire at school. Oliver said to me to go outside. Oliver's hair got burnt, so now he has no hair.

Georgia Browning (9)

Highgate Primary Academy, Goldthorpe

Sundown Adventureland

Dear Diary,

We arrived and I was bored because there was a circle and I thought that was it. But then we went on a ride and I loved it. We went to the Angry Birds park. We went on a second ride and then my favourite one: Bouncy Pigs. It went up and down and it made my belly go funny, so I screamed. After a couple of rides, it was raining so we went in a play area for dinner. Then it started raining again, so we went on the really big slide in the play area. When we were going home, it was thunderstorming!

Phoebe Deakin (8)

Highgate Primary Academy, Goldthorpe

The Incredible Diary Of Harley Quinn

Dear Diary,

In the beginning, me and the others were put in jail. We got dragged in wheelchairs. Next, we got sent in a helicopter on a mission. Then Joker texted me: 'I'm coming soon'.

One hour later, me and the others started to kill the zombies. Then I got another text: 'I'm nearly there'.

Three hours later, I jumped into the helicopter. Next, I jumped out and Joker arrived.

Isabella Frost (10)

Highgate Primary Academy, Goldthorpe

All About My Childhood

Dear Diary,

When I was younger, I had a lot of night terrors in my old house for about three or four years. I was very scared. So, when I was very scared, I went into my mum and dad's room.

They said there was nothing there, but I said there was. Then my mum and dad put me back to bed. When I fell back asleep, it happened again, so I kept on going in their room and they put me back to bed.

Beau-James Ash (9)

Highgate Primary Academy, Goldthorpe

The Strange Day

Dear Diary,

Yesterday was a plain old Monday. But I didn't know what was coming. I went to school at a normal time and came back as normal.

When I got home, I sat down to do my homework but, suddenly, a bright light shone through my window and then I blacked out. The next morning, I didn't remember anything, so I got ready for school.

Noah Mallinson (9)

Highgate Primary Academy, Goldthorpe

The Bar At A Competition

Dear Diary,

Yesterday was the worst day ever! I got covered in white chalk. Also, people kept on swinging on me, jumping on me and putting powder on me! Urgh! They have no manners. I hate my job. When they are gone the coaches put me away in a dusty, old room with my friends.

Today I know I'm going to get treated badly, everyone is counting on me. Finally, some respect from these fools! I was scared I was going to mess them up. What happens if my bolts come loose? If they lose it all rests on me.

Mia Franklin (10)
Holbrook Primary School, Bridgemary

The Day I Woke Up In A Fairy Tale

Dear Diary,

My day has been interesting. First off, it started with me waking up in a different place from home. It was sunny and summer and I was surrounded by flowers and trees. It was like a special forest. I got up and stood there staring at my surroundings, it was magical. All of a sudden, I saw something peeking from out behind the tree. I decided to follow it. It went far through the bushes and trees and through the meadows...

Caelyn Lane (10)

Holbrook Primary School, Bridgemary

Even At Home, Amazing Things Can Happen

Dear Diary,

Hi, my name is Thomas the Tank Engine and I will tell you about the dynamic time I have with a boy every day!

It happened when I was bought by a boy called Matthew. Since then, he plays with us either in the living room or bedroom. We are as cheerful as a lark after Matthew is dropped off to school because we are all alive and with other engines to play together like Toy Story until Matthew comes back home. He is gentle and kind, we want to stay even longer!

The best day is when Matthew changes our characters, like a fancy dress party! He uses masking tape and wraps it around our bodies. It tickles a bit but we do not mind at all!

Straight away as Matthew comes back home he starts looking for his tools and gets busy disassembling or assembling us. We love being assembled even better because it means we are alive again and if our motor is in working order, he did fantastic! We will have even more adventures here from now on.

Matthew Trzcinski (11)

Holy Family Catholic Primary School, West Acton

Cleo's Puppy Gets Lost

Dear Diary,

Today I woke up and got breakfast for me and my dog Pip. After breakfast, I got my clothes on and brushed my teeth. Then when I put the TV on I put Pip's fave show on.

I said, "Pip! I'm putting your fave show on!" Pip usually comes but she didn't! "Pip, where are you?" I shouted. "Pip is lost! Oh no!" I cried.

I looked behind a cushion, she wasn't there, so I looked in the kitchen, everywhere but she wasn't there. Today was not a very good day, it was a bad day, a very bad day! *What if my mum finds out? I am going to be in big trouble!* I thought. Then I heard a bark!

"Oh! That must be Pip." I followed the barking sound and found Pip. "Really Pip? You were under the sofa all along. Wait, where is Princess?" I asked.

Pip shook her head.

"Oh no! Now Princess is lost so now that's why I didn't see her this morning."

But Princess was under the sofa as well. Well, I didn't look there.

Zoe Vaughan (8)
Hopton Primary School, Hopton

Sports Day

Dear Diary,

On sports day Bella sneakily ate doughnuts because Bella loves doughnuts. Oh, I forgot, I am ten years old. When we were doing our sports day in school it was sunny then an hour later it rained and started raining more. Then I had a snack at sports day then I had to do more activities then we did a running race and I was fifth.

Until tomorrow.

Ellina Gooda (8)

Hopton Primary School, Hopton

Hard Luck

Dear Diary,

Mom's always saying that friends will come and go but family is forever. Well, if that's true, I could be in for a rough ride.

I mean I love my family and all, but I'm just not sure we were meant to live together. Maybe it'll be better later on when we're all in different houses and only see each other on holidays, but right now things are just a little dicey.

Frank Grzela (9)
Hunsbury Park Primary School, Camp Hill

The Best Days Of My Life

Dear Diary,

I have done lots of fun stuff and played with my friends but the best days of my life are when we have school trips and that's not all. Another few days I like are the chilly snowboard days. If you want to know more, I'll tell you one more thing. I love the sunny days too and that's everything about me.

Andrew Lazar (8)

Hunsbury Park Primary School, Camp Hill

Diary

Dear Diary,

I woke up at 8:13 and brushed my teeth, had breakfast and washed my face. My mum bought a bicycle at the car boot where people sold goodies and I rode it all the way home. I had lunch and played on the phone's games before bedtime.

Kofi Ofosu Sarpong (8)

Hunsbury Park Primary School, Camp Hill

Frog

Dear Diary,
Before I left to vacation in China, in my pool something amazing happened. A tadpole appeared, not one but twenty! Then, when I got back home, they hatched. I walked into my garden, the frog wanted me to be their leader.

Nicola Krasinska (10)
Hunsbury Park Primary School, Camp Hill

The Car Crash

Dear Diary,

My name is Amelia and I am nine years old, I have blue eyes, blonde hair and my favourite colours are green and pink.

I got into a big car crash and it happened on the A45. I felt scared, worried and threatened.

Amelia Bell (9)

Hunsbury Park Primary School, Camp Hill

The Diary Of Riley

An extract

Dear Diary,

It was Monday 13th August 2021 and it was the biggest day of my little puppy life. I was about to get adopted. I was *so* excited. I was talking about it with my sisters all morning, they were getting a bit annoyed. I was sprinting around my little pen so excited, but then someone was walking through the gate and coming over to me and I froze with nerves. This little girl and I think her mum and um... grandma... well, they're hot dogs so I'm not too sure, but anyway, I was still frozen and I needed to pull myself together. I stood up tall but then I pooped and started barking and jumping with joy. The little girl picked me up, it was like Cupid hit me, I knew we were going to be best friends for life. She took me to a big thing with wheels, she opened a door and put me in like a car seat for dogs. I fell asleep for a long time, dreaming of all the fun adventures we would have. I woke up and tried to climb out of the box seat thing but the girl put me back in. I fell asleep again and this time when I woke up I was getting lifted out of the car seat box thing and into a tall building. The little girl put me down and petted me and hugged me but the weird thing was she called me 'Riley'. *I loved it.*

I ran over and explored the house, I think that's what it's called. *So* many new sniffs. I ran over to the little girl and jumped all over her, she laughed so hard it made me more excited.

Esme Murray (11)
Kettins Primary School, Kettins

The Diary Of Mario

Dear Diary,
Today Donkey Kong's army of monkeys came to attack the kingdom. I was running to the castle when Donkey Kong jumped onto the path. My red suit and my blue overalls were drenched in sweat. Just when I thought I couldn't run anymore, Yoshi jumped out with a crowd of toads. I jumped on his back. He was way faster.
I got to the castle. I opened the door but the princess was not there.

Henry Rayner (8)
Kimbolton St James' CE Primary School, Kimbolton

Frozen Sleepover

Dear Diary,

Hello, I am in a room because my friend is coming over today for a sleepover. I am in my room getting ready and finding a game we can play. Maybe we can play swingball.

I was jumping with excitement until she finally arrived. We had so much fun with the game. She cheated so when she came into my room I froze her. When she said sorry I unfroze her. She went home in the morning and then I went into the pool.

Alisha Addicott (8)
Kingsmoor Primary School, Bawdrip

Pikachu Is Lost

Dear Diary,
I was lost in a forest. Let me tell you how that happened. So one day ago Ash and I were out and we went into a forest but then Ash was nowhere to be found and I was nowhere to be found. Ash was looking for me and he found me and we went home.

Kasie-Leigh Anderson (9)
Knockmore Primary School, Lisburn

Diary Of Finley Huseltine

Dear Diary,

I went to bed at 10pm. I woke up at 10am, then I had breakfast, then went to school and learned about Jesus and when he was born. I said, "How?" and my teacher said, "He was created."

I said, "Can we write a sentence about Jesus?" She said, "Yes."

I said, "All right." Then we went for dinner, then it was playtime and then I started running. My brother and my friend went for a bike ride. I said, "Can I come too?" They said no. I was upset, so I followed them and I found out they were meeting someone. He was not allowed to. I told my dad and my mum, we had to go home, he got told off.

Finley Huseltine (10)

Lakes Primary School, Redcar

The Worst Day Of My Life

Dear Diary,

Six days after Christmas, my and Mum were making cookies when Dad came in from work. He said, "I've had a trash day."

"We had a great day. Didn't we, Lily?" said Mum nicely.

"I don't care what day you've had. Anyway..." Dad just went on about work for another twenty to thirty minutes.

Later that day I was in bed, still awake when I heard shouting downstairs. It unexpectedly shattered me. I burst into tears. All of a sudden I heard a scream and a bang. I got up and ran downstairs. I saw the most horrifying thing ever... I saw my mum's body and my dad standing over her. With no delay, I rang the police. In the blink of an eye, it all went away. My dad was arrested and my mum was dead. What would happen to me? Where would I live?

Two days later, I was in foster care. I've had six homes already. I'm now with the Waits family. It's been hard adjusting but I'm happy. Me and the Waits spent Christmas together and they adopted me.

Rosie Rayner (11)

Langtree Community School, Langtree

130

An Old Man

Dear Diary,

Once upon a time in a plane there lived an old man who didn't like people. He flew his plane once a week.

He was taking off one day and as he was in the sky the plane stopped. He had to jump. He couldn't find his parachute. As the plane was rotating his parachute fell out so he grabbed it and put it on. He was going 100mph.

Smash! He landed in a cave. He was trapped. A dog looked at him and attacked him.

Chester Taylor-Coleman (10)

Langtree Community School, Langtree

Battle Royale

Dear Diary,

Today has been the craziest day ever. It all began when I was playing Pac-Man and it made me want to play Fortnite and then all of a sudden I got sucked into the game. It felt quite cool. All Fortnite people vs Stone so I went and saw what was going on but Epic Games kept telling me not to go to the war but I ignored them and I grabbed a gun and joined.

It was an intense war but we were winning because it was one million vs one! It looked easy but it was hard. Stone is strong but not stronger than us. It was a tough-fought battle with Stone whipping one-half of the team but at the start, we didn't know that Jonsey's dad was secretly walking with her. But then V-Bucks fell from the sky and then we bought a bigger army but there were so many clones. Because I won I got my own icon skin.

Brax Pritchard (9)

Laughton Junior & Infant School, Laughton-En-Le-Morthen

Bill Kaulitz And Tom Kaulitz

Dear Diary,

Today I met my favourite band Tokio Hotel. Before the song 'Monsoon' started Bill and Tom looked nervous and scared. Suddenly, the whole crowd screamed and yelled and that's when the song started and a happy feeling went down my spine and I started to sing along to the song.

A minute later, the song stopped and that's when I went backstage. Tom and Bill gave me a hug and they started to teach me some German because they are German - I loved it! On my way home now and I got McDonald's.

From Demie.

Demie Smith (10)

Margaretting CE (VC) Primary School, Margaretting

The Incredible Diary Of Mario

Dear Diary,

I have just lost my brother, Luigi. He has gone missing from a sewer in Brooklyn. We went through a portal. I went to a place called the Mushroom Kingdom but my brother wasn't as lucky as me, he went to the dark realms, we're under Bowser's control! I must convince the mighty Cranky Kong to help us to defeat Bowser.

When I got there I met a crazy monkey who took me to Cranky Kong. He told me that the king was very mean and never let anybody get his army because he believed they were the best in the world.

When I got there I saw Cranky Kong. He said I could only get his army by beating his son. When I saw his son two hours later he was a four-foot-tall monkey with a six-pack but if this is what it took to get Luigi I would do... I had to prepare for the fight of my life...

Aadam Azeem (9)

Mayfield Preparatory School, Walsall

The Incredible Diary Of Link

Dear Diary,

Today was stressful. I had made my way from the divine beast, Rito. I defeated Windblight Ganon. The best thing was I had found all the abilities for defeating Ganon. The castle was far so I called my horse, Epona, and we made our way. As we got closer guardians came into sight. We snuck past into the gates straight into the throne room. There was a big cacoon that I shot with an arrow and the cacoon broke the floor and our battlefield was set. Ganon appeared and I took the sword that seals darkness and my shield and started the fight. The swords crashed and shields clashed. It was painful but I defeated him. Princess Zelda was freed and my quest was over.

Goodbye, and I shall write to you again.

Link.

Aydin Shan (9)

Mayfield Preparatory School, Walsall

Alien Saves Other Aliens

Dear Diary,

Today was the best day ever. Let me tell you...

Me and my friend were chilling in the UFO when we saw a homeless kid who was severely injured on the floor. He wasn't moving so I told Bob to use the sucker which would such the kid up into the UFO.

He started to speak our alien language and the kid understood us. We asked the kid to tell us his name.

He said, "My name is Tommy."

I took Bob to a different room and said, "Do you think this could be Tommy that we haven't seen in years?"

Bob said, "I was thinking the exact same thing."

I said, "Should we see how he ended up in the middle of nowhere or should we do the tests first?"

"We should do the tests because then we will know whether he is human or alien."

We put him in a coma and left him there for twenty minutes. Then we got him up. The tests which told you if you were an alien or human came back positive. I asked some questions.

The first one was, "How did you end up like this?" Tommy said, "I was coming back to the alien station and there were men with guns who said, "Shoot!" That's how I ended up here."

Kyle Deeble (10)

Mill Lodge Primary School, Shirley

Snowy's Frozen Adventure

Dear Diary,

I had the best adventure. Me and my friends were walking in the snow. We were going to save summer because if we didn't save summer our land would be frozen forever. There were human people living on our land.

"I know how to bring back summer," I said, "we just have to find a special potion."

We walked and walked until we found it. We ran back and splashed it on the floor of the Scendyly Church. All the snow and ice disappeared. We were the best heroes in one hundred years. Pretty much everyone was our friend.

Lucas Moss (8)

Mill Lodge Primary School, Shirley

The Fused Adventure

Dear Diary,

I had the weirdest day of my life. I woke up from my amazing sleep. My best friend, Chica, called me and a portal showed up! I obviously jumped in.

I felt a flash go through my eyes and I was in the Stone Age! I found some cavemen but I forgot they didn't speak English.

Later that night, I found a cave with the cavemen inside! They let me in but another portal took me to Hawaii!

When I was there, I found my family!

Luca Cox (9)

Mill Lodge Primary School, Shirley

Annabella's Magical Adventure

An extract

Dear Diary,

I was really sad because my sister was going to the forest with her friend.

The next day I stayed at home. Then I heard a knock at the door. I thought that must be my sister. I rushed downstairs and opened the door but it was her friend that went to the forest with my sister, but my sister wasn't there.

My sister's friend said, "Your sister is badly injured." Mammy rushed to the door. "Don't worry, she is at the hospital."

I heard there were a lot of people getting injured in the forest. I had to go and find out what was happening. I was really scared but I had to do it. When I was little I got a gem of powers given to me. I packed the gem and food and water in the ugliest bag and headed out.

I had to stop at the school and tell the teacher I wouldn't be at school for a while but I didn't tell her why. Then I headed for the forest which was a long way away.

I was really tired and exhausted and it was dusk, so I settled beside a tree and went to sleep because I was really worried about my sister.

Eventually I got to sleep but that didn't last long. A wolf was attacking someone. I took a deep breath and said, "I can do this."

I had to save the girl from the wolf. So I tried really hard because the wolf was big and I was small but I saved her and we became friends.

Time went by and my sister got better.

Sinéad Hannon (9)

Millquarter Primary School, Toomebridge

Girl Asks Boy

Friday 15th January
Dear Diary,
Today was the worst day ever! So first mean girl Emma stole my French books and I was late to class. Two after-school detentions but I was still happy I got to go to the girl-ask-boy winter dance. I am going to ask my crush Ben, I hope he says yes. I am going dress shopping with my two BFFs Larna and Zara.

Saturday 16th January
Dear Diary,
Today I am going dress shopping and I am going to text Ben at some point today. I think I found the perfect dress, it is pale blue with white high heels and a blue purse. I am texting Ben now. I hope he says yes. Got to go, bye.

Sunday 17th January
Dear Diary,
OMG OMG OMG, he actually said yes. I have to go!

Orla McGrogan (9)
Millquarter Primary School, Toomebridge

The Secret Of Kylie's Diary

Dear Diary,

My name is Kylie and I just moved to a new school. Everyone keeps bullying me in school and even the teachers don't like me and there is this mean girl in my school, she is really mean. When we were in class, writing a story, she was copying me and she told me off. At lunchtime, I didn't want to eat my lunch and I was crying in the bathroom.

Every time it was lunchtime, I was always crying in the bathroom. But one day, there was really something that cheesed me off. Chelsea, the mean girl, pushed me off my chair and everyone was laughing at me, and I was bullied every single day. Until, one day, everything changed and I wasn't bullied anymore...

Simisola Amusa (9)

Moredon Primary & Nursery School, Moredon

Life In Lego City

Dear Diary,

Today in Lego City, I met my friends at a delicious diner. We all ate a massive burger which was magnificent. It had pickles, beef, cheese and sesame seeds. After we all ate, I went outside and it was so sunny that I had to wear my colourful sunglasses. It was okay because I love to wear them.

Me and my friends went to get ice poles from the best ice cream seller in Lego City, Edds ice cream! As soon as we brought them, I licked and licked and licked until it was gone. After I'd eaten my ice pole I saw some superheroes defeating a colossal cat that was destroying the city. It was so cool. The best part of today was when I got to see and meet Superman, Batman and Aquaman!

Bye! John.

Frankie Little (10)

Muscliff Primary School, Bournemouth

The Lonely Girl

Dear Diary,

Today, was an incredible day. It all started with a red magical pencil. I was lonely and had nobody to play with, so I drew a door that took me to a magical place... I walked through a colourful forest that took me to a river running through it, I then drew a boat to take me down the river. As I went down through the river it led me to a huge beautiful kingdom. As I got nearer to the kingdom there were a lot of guards surrounding the grounds, but they were all very nice and friendly. Then as I was upon the kingdom I looked across and noticed a waterfall fast approaching! But unfortunately, it was too late and I had no idea what to do at that point as I was already falling! So, I quickly got the magic pen out and drew a big, bright hot air balloon, which I quickly jumped on and it flew away towards the peaceful, calm and cloudy sky, with the magic kingdom now gone and in the distance.

From the Lonely Girl.

Sonny Mee (10)
North Petherton Community Primary School, North Petherton

Lonely Girl's Diary

Dear Diary,

Today was an incredible day. Filled with adventure and joy. I was armed with only a mysterious and magical red crayon. I was starting an extraordinary journey that nobody had been on before, leaving my grey, miserable and dull city behind me. With each line of my crayon, I breathed life into a magical door leading me to places nobody had seen before.

It all started when I felt like I was invisible. No one would play with me. I asked my family, but they were all too busy to play. So, I walked into my room, thinking what I could do, my cat was sleeping in my room but got up and walked away. As I sat there in my bed, I noticed my cat left a magical red crayon behind. As I got out of my bed, I picked up the crayon and I started drawing a door that would lead to a secret dimension.

As I entered the mysterious place, I was in the middle of the woods. I saw a jetty nearby, so I ran over to it and I drew a boat to go on an adventure. I came upon a massive castle, there were guards everywhere. As I was making my way into the castle, all the guards started waving at me and saying hello. I was still following the path until I came to a fountain, so I drew a hot air balloon to catch me.

From the Lonely Girl.

Isla Cole (10)

North Petherton Community Primary School, North Petherton

A Lonely Adventure...

Dear Diary,

I am afraid that my adventure is coming to an end; a lot of breathtaking things have happened.

Armed with only one red crayon, secrets have whispered in the unknown. An enchanted door, a mythical purple bird; but the most unbelievable thing, a magical red crayon.

Now I am here, on a red carpet, flying with the bird. I thought I would give her a name, so I thought Violet because it suits her. While flying on the red carpet, underneath me stood a beautifully lit town. We flew across the town and the sky had gone a darker lilac and then turned to dusk. We finally landed (by we I meant me, because Violet is a fast flyer). Furthermore, I opened the door which was in a tree. Violet went in first. Then I crawled in. Surprisingly, I went in a tree, came out of a letterbox. Also, Violet flew out so quickly that she went to who I think is her owner. I noticed that he also had a crayon but purple. We started drawing something that turned into a bike.

Now, I am not a lonely girl. I have a friend to play with and to trust.

Goodbye, Diary, see you tomorrow...

Liliana B (11)

North Petherton Community Primary School, North Petherton

The Lonely Girl

Dear Diary,
Today started as a miserable day.
I went on a journey with my red pen which made my dreams come true. It all started with the magical door which led to an enchanted forest with a river running through. I used my red pen to draw the boat which took me to a kingdom guarded by knights in shining armour. They welcomed me into their big, gigantic castle. I saw a purple bird and some evil people in the kingdom and I got past all the guards and released the purple bird.
From the lonely girl.

Mason Nixon (10)
North Petherton Community Primary School, North Petherton

Brother Cuthbert

Tiw 793 CE, Dear Diary,
Today is our special day, do you know why?
Everyone in our spectacular home will come
together and pray to our worshipped God for all
our wonderful treasures. It was a very stormy day.
After praying, we went to clean.

Woden 793 CE, Dear Diary,
After cleaning, I heard a massive bang and
everyone screaming in fear. I didn't know what to
do, so I hid in the nearest bush. I came out of the
bush and found that all my family were dead. Not
a very good sight. I was devastated, but I have to
fight to survive. I got caught coming out of the
bush. They dragged me to the boat.

Thanor 793 CE, Dear Diary,
In the boat, I was sailing across the river. I tried to
grab the valuables off the boat and run away, but
they caught me. Goodbye, diary.

Lilly-Mae Fox (9)
Outwood Primary Academy Bell Lane, Ackworth

The Disaster Of Bikini Bottom

Dear Diary,

As I was working the fryer, Mr. Krabs came and told me to look at the news. As I walked to the TV everybody watching looked terrified like they had seen a ghost. Once I approached the TV I saw a flash warning of a sandstorm. I looked outside, nothing was happening yet. I thought maybe they were wrong but right when I thought that, the Krusty Krab went into lockdown mode. That hasn't happened for over five years. I was starting to be scared, it wasn't just me who was scared, Squidward was panicking because he had his clarinet recital. The Krusty Krab shook and shook like never before. The worst sandstorm on record. Plus we were running out of food. I tried to ask Mr. Krabs for help but he was too busy protecting his money. I was hoping this was all a dream. I kept on pinching myself, just hoping. I was sure it was the end, that's when things started to break but then out of nowhere, the TV came on saying it was the end of the sandstorm. I couldn't have been more glad. I ran outside. The damage it did to our city was tremendous, so I ran to my house that luckily was still standing.

Max Roberts (10)

Pelsall Village School, Pelsall

A Day In The Life Of A Pencil In Nursery

Dear Diary,

In the cold, breezy winter, all the hooligans come back to school. Ugh, honestly, I just hate those nursery kids. They always chew me, bite me, and the worst one: they put me in the horrid pencil sharpeners.

Let's think on the good side, at least I get a fresh haircut every two seconds because they always break my head (tip of the pencil). Wish me luck for art next session. Pray for me! Finish this tomorrow, bye!

Dear Diary,

I'm still traumatised from that Art lesson. It was horrid! They kept eating me, throwing me on the floor, and the worst: putting me in paint! Like, how would a human being produce that much action? And they are little! Not even my grandma could do that action when she was 150. OMG, if I have to deal with them again tomorrow then I'm quitting my job! Give me strength...

Fatimah Zeidan (10)

Queen's Park Primary School, Westminster

Let The Cat Out Of The Bag

Dear Diary,

Today was weird, confusing and many other funny emotions. In the morning I was putting my books into my bookbag and left it open on the floor. My cat crawled in and when I got to school she jumped out! A mixture of emotions came to my mind as I tried not to panic. I chased her around the *entire school.* It was exhausting! I'm probably the only person who has run around the entire school. I came into a classroom and I saw poo everywhere (and wee). But finally, in the Year 5 classroom, I found her, shaking. The school called my parents and they took her home. I wish I could go with her. *I am going to get killed at home!*

Layla Omar (11)

Riverside Primary School, Barking

When I Met Bobby

We have always wondered if there was another planet other than Earth... Let me take you back to the time I met Bobby and his older sister, Bob. It was just an ordinary day at high school and as I came I was petrified to see two bald students. One looked like the other and both looked unfocused. I heard their names were Bob and Bobby.

"Bahahaha!"

Everyone followed with, "Hahahaha!"

Bobby looked very embarrassed but Bob was simply staring out the window. What if... Just then Bobby asked to go to the bathroom.

Since I knew where he sat I placed something on his seat and got a microphone. As he was about to sit down everyone giggled. *Pppppppppfffffffftttt!*

I landed in detention. Yeah, I was a weirdo then.

Another time I got my pet spider and said it was for show 'n' tell. I pretended to let it out and they went wild. And that is how we met.

Anjali Raithatha (9)

Rosedale Primary School, Hayes

How I Met Cristiano Ronaldo

Dear Diary,

You won't believe what happened two days ago! A well-known footballer met me at a pizza shop (called Domino's). We had a very long discussion. When my pizza was ready to pick up he invited me for dinner with his family. When I got there the house was massive and he told me that when he was a small kid he had to go through surgery because he had a heart problem.

He only had two choices, to go through surgery that may kill him or never play football ever again. Of course, he chose the surgery. I thought to myself, *that had to be painful.*

Then I had the best idea ever, why not go to his upcoming football match? I went and he scored his 800th goal. I had another idea. I went to his house and had a party to celebrate his 800th goal.

I will update you soon. Bye.

Matias Baintan (10)

Rosedale Primary School, Hayes

My First Time On A Plane

Dear Diary,

You won't believe what my parents told me yesterday. They told me that we were going to Turkey by plane. I was shocked. Also, our flight is tomorrow.

Dear Diary,

We went to the airport and boarded. As soon as I got to my seat I munched on all the snacks. Two hours later, the flight attendants gave me food and it was delicious.

An hour after, we landed. We went to an aquarium which was so enigmatic and elegant. There were also people who were in the fish tank. It was so cool! We saw a penguin show and also got to see the penguins swim.

On the way back to the hotel I saw a lot of stray animals. I was astonished and sad.

See you later, Diary!

Yasmin Islam (10)

Rosedale Primary School, Hayes

The Sad Diary Of Mort's Life

Dear Diary,

This morning I woke up. I got dressed, brushed my teeth and the kids came because my mum is a childminder. Chester, Lahla and Arthur came to the daycare a few minutes late! I went to school.

In literacy, I was really bad. In maths, I got everything correct and then I went to break. I went back in and after school, I went home with my nan. I was in the lounge and saw Mum and Dad looking very upset. My nan left. I went over and said, "What's wrong?"

Then Mum said, "Mort has died."

I started to cry for two hours on and off. We spoke about what we did with Mort.

Harrison Parker Leitch (8)

Samares Primary School, St Clement

Diary Of Dippy Jeff

Dear Diary,

I was walking down my street when it started to get sunny to cold. But then my bullies came, surrounding me and said, "Hello, we're here to take you somewhere, it's a surprise."

"Surprise, it's a brand-new secret house, how do you like it, Jeff?"

"Woah, thank you so much, I will never ruin it."

"Okay, well, perfect, we will ruin it!"

I said, "I'm not letting you bullies in the gaming room to ruin the gaming ruin, so get out of my house before I kick you out."

"Oh no, we're not getting out of your house."

"Okay, I'm kicking you out!" I said.

Bethany Norman (8)

Sculthorpe CE Primary School, Sculthorpe

Best Day Ever!

Dear Diary,

I went to the airport and the pilot shouted, "Let Kayla Derrett in first class!" and I went on a soft comfy bed and I ate yummy sugary shortbread and melty chocolate and I felt so special. Then I arrived at a beautiful city called Hawaii and when I landed in Hawaii I headed straight to the beach. There were lots of people at the beach. The sea was blue and clean and the sand was yellow, crunchy and calm. After, I went to a restaurant called Foody Friday 4Ever and I got a Big Tasty. A Big Tasty has lettuce, tomatoes, steak, cheese and sauce. It was so good and yummy. Then I went to my clean, big hotel and ordered a Nutella fudge brownie. Then I got into my fluffy Stitch pyjamas and went to bed.

Kayla Derrett (9)
Seaton School, Aberdeen

The Incredible Diary Of Grog Strongjaw

Dear Diary,

We were in a meeting with the council. We were being told to kill some monster. Then a lady took us to a hill. The lady left us to walk up the hill. Halfway up the hill was a little town. I suddenly realised that the town was in ruins. Then they said we would kill the monster.

"You mean the dragon," said a kid.

So we went up to the hillside but a dragon came and breathed lightning. I ran towards the dragon with my axe and I attacked the dragon but it left.

Noah Duncan (11)

Southmuir Primary School, Kirriemuir

The Diary Of Arasho

Dear Diary,

I had a terrible day but when I went to school they said, "There is no school."

"What? Is this true? Where are the teachers?"

"On holiday."

"What? When there is school? This is not good."

Maybe it will be better tomorrow.

Awais Ali (10)

St Andrew's CE Primary School, Whitmore Reans

A Sour Lemon, Yuck!

Dear Diary,

Poof! I found myself in a bag of lemons. I feel so happy but... an alien-type creature with stick-like hands, well... the sticks were on the hands, they picked me up and sniffed me on the cheek! And said, "Yuck!" Then she peeled me open, like who does she think she is to peel me! So rude, I just can't believe it. I wanted to throw up my hands, but... I realised I didn't have any! After that she licked me! The audacity! I got so mad. So I decided to fight her. *Boom!* I was winning, yippee, ha! That idiot didn't win against a lemon! Hehe, but... just then I went down a slippery tube and into a big, red area. Suddenly I saw my friends (the sweet lemons). Yay! I missed them. I ran and gave them a big hug. I saw the light that went into a big swimming pool. Then down a hatch, then into a big brown and smelly area and there was a ladder and we crawled out. We all shouted, "We're free!"

Abigail Starrs (9)
St Brigid's Primary School, Londonderry

Charlie The Cheeky Nugget

Dear Diary,

One day I was in the freezer. Then it was time. Time to go in the big bad pan! I was so scared, I was shaking. I made a plan to escape the pan. Every second I was getting hotter and hotter. I climbed out and said, "Excuse me, I'm not trying to be rude or anything, but why is your pan so crusty, dusty, musty?" I shouted in a sassy tone.

I ran because I didn't want anyone to see me. I sassily walked into B&M. I thought it was a beauty aisle but when I walked into the make-up aisle I shouted in a sassy tone, "OMG, it's make-up!"

When I was going to the checkout, I got eaten by girls named Priya, Abi and Georgia. I died that night at midnight.

What a tragedy!

RIP Charlie the cheeky chicken nugget.

Priya McEmerson (9)

St Brigid's Primary School, Londonderry

A Hero That Saved A Kid's Life

Dear Diary,

Kabam! I just turned into a hero! So there was a kid walking on the pathway then he tripped then I went up to him. I said, "Are you okay?"

He said, "Yes I am but my elbow and my ankles are really sore."

I said, "Stay there, I will get a bandage and supplies."

"I'm back, I will put the bandage on you now."

"Yay! My ankle and my elbow don't hurt anymore."

He got back up, started walking and he is fine now. After he turned his back I used my superpowers and flew into a car.

Dean McIntyre (9)

St Brigid's Primary School, Londonderry

The New Kid

An extract

Dear Diary,

Hey, how are you? Today was the best day of my life! So, let me tell you about it. It all started when I walked into the classroom and I saw my teacher. She was called Ms Laisha. Ms Laisha was our new form teacher until December.

She said, "Good morning, I am..." blah, blah, blah. She said we should introduce ourselves and say something about ourselves and what we like to do.

I said, "Hi, my name is Sapphela and I am fifteen years old. I have a disease called Cystic Fibrosis, which is caused when there is too much mucus in your lungs."

"She has... I don't know, who cares what she has? It's her lifetime job to have it, ha!" Isabell shouted out to the whole class.

Everybody started laughing. I couldn't help but stand up for myself and say, "Unlike you, I am lucky to have a lifetime job." I said it nicely. She didn't say a word after that and the whole class went silent. "Victory!" I screamed.

"Okay, that's enough. Next!" the teacher said. I was so embarrassed.

Suddenly, with a loud bang, a boy burst through the door. "What in the world? He's the new kid!" everybody said. Except for me, all I could say in my head was, *he's so familiar... but anyway, let's focus. Wait! He's Kylan from primary school! My old best friend.* His name was Kylan Smith. Yep, I remembered him, but he had changed a lot.

Samuela Oppong (10)

St Edward's Catholic Primary School, Upton Park

The Diary Of The Depressed Sister

Dear Diary,

My name is Leah Jackson Fiona. I am fourteen years old and I go to St Bede's. Today was not that bad actually. I got 75% on my maths test.

I decided to go on a mission to find my missing sister. She had been missing for four years. In 2019, my sister went on a walk with her friends. She somehow got lost... I packed my stuff to find my eleven-year-old sister. I saw signs and felt that she was calling me. Weird and coincidence?

Hello Diary,

Today was okay. I mean, it wasn't the best but I could deal with it. My 'best friends' ignored me again. I couldn't stop thinking about my sister. Her name was Maria Jackson Fiona.

"Leah, get down here now! We need to go!" shouted Michael.

Oh, that's my brother, Michael. He can be a bit shouty sometimes.

"Come on, I don't want to be late! Leah!" yelled Michael.

I tried to ignore him and covered my ears until it all went silent and heard the door slam...

Now I'll tell you where it happened. It happened in a haunted abandoned city, located in Los Angeles. I mean she loved haunted movies. I packed and left the house to find my sister.

Five hours later, I arrived at the place. It felt so haunted. I felt the cold breeze touching the edge of my shoulder. Leaves crunching, birds chirping, water dripping. I started to search for clues my sister could've left. Suddenly, I found her backpack. I followed a path and found a shed. I broke in and found a girl hiding in the corner. "Maria...?" I whispered. She turned around and recognised me. She was covered in bruises and big scars all around her body. "Leah? I-i-is that you?" she stammered. "We need to go home before anyone catches you..." I said. I took her home before anyone saw me.

Kezia Celestino (11)
St Joseph's Catholic Primary School, Redhill

Cloud Village

An extract

Dear Diary,

I couldn't believe what happened today! It was the biggest adventure of my life. But at the same time, the most unreasonable, most annoying week of my life. I still didn't understand why she chose me to find all of it. Like, what have I ever done to deserve all of that? What have I shown to make them think I could find trillions of billions of the dragon currency, crystal coins?

You probably don't know a thing I'm talking about. Sorry if you want to find out what I'm saying though, read on, obviously...

So really, what happened is this. As normal, I went to work at Crystal Village Banks. As I glanced through the large, modern window at the front of the building, I saw a sight that made me want to turn around and go home. Reluctantly, I stepped inside and as I went in, the world stopped moving. Coffee cups slipped out of my hands and dropped to the floor. Papers flew in the air and everyone just stopped and stared for a while. That was until Mrs Banks came down.

"Sky! Look everybody, stay here," she enthusiastically screamed even though everyone was already staring at me.

My brain still hadn't processed that fully so I said, "Pardon?"

I nearly fainted when I first heard what I had to do. But to be honest, it was predictable. The banks had been robbed of all of their crystal coins but the part that nearly made me faint was the fact that everyone had nominated me to find and/or gain all the crystal coins back! Can you believe it? But by far, the fact that I only had twenty-four hours to find them was the craziest thing. Then I thought to myself, *how am I supposed to find the crystal coins when I'm the one who basically lost them?*

Aizah Nadeem (10)

St Joseph's Catholic Primary School, Redhill

My Diary

An extract

Dear Diary,

Oh my goodness! I've never witnessed such a chaotic, terrifying, near-death, horrific but terrific, horrible-ish mission ever done by me. Yes, I know what you're thinking, how can I, a kluflyfle master still be alive after the... Here's what really happened...

I woke up late. Alarm clock buzzing, ran to school and that's about it. My everyday life is an endless recap. Only that was an extra-not ordinary day, an unexpected one...

The next case and literally the only case of tracking money contained suitcases. The man was wearing a black jacket, black boots and tried to look cool, which he didn't. Next, he went on his motorcycle and arrived at the bank. He stole the money suitcases and reached his and the gang of thieves' hideout. By the time me and my community's organisation were already hunting down the money, suitcases and obviously the gang of thieves, they were hacking into our system. Me and my organisation had to head out. There was no choice...

We ended them somehow. *Pow! Kapow! Boom! Strike!* Minutes away from collapsing, they tried to head out but we cornered them knowing there was more harm ahead of us. They shot the bullet into the building's glass. The bullet, inches away from my face, soared through the sky. We attacked them with all our might and they collapsed. Without warning, we were notified that we won. Me and my sister seized the moment with an unlimited victory.

My little siblings stayed at home with the babysitter whilst me, Michelle (my older sister), Amanda and Kris (my mum and dad) were standing in a nearly demolished urban city. No one can actually find out that it was us, right? Wait, right? Huh? Wait, wait, what?

Khadija Asif (10)
St Joseph's Catholic Primary School, Redhill

My Spy Diary

An extract

Dear Diary,

Today was a typical Tuesday but my chest hurts, there are blisters around both my hands, my knees are bleeding badly and there are scratches all over my body. Surely you'd be thinking how a tiny thirteen-year-old unpopular girl became a fully trained spy. Well, I can tell you the story...

It all started when I was a baby. I was born with a necklace, apparently. My real parents died in a car crash so I was stuck with my adoptive parents, who are nice but I am also stuck with my spoiled, lazy, rude and vain adopted sister. On the bright side, I have both my real brothers with me.

I was with my sister because she wanted me to go with her while she was shopping with her friends. I saw an unoccupied watch and took it.

When I got home it started beeping. Soon, a man started talking. I didn't listen until I heard, "The prime minister Linsy Lauren's husband has been kidnapped..."

Soon I panicked. I got a backpack full of weapons. I thought to myself, *I am on a mission*. As I stepped out of the house, I nearly slipped because of my heavy weapons.

I took the bag off and remembered I hadn't had any breakfast. Quickly, I ran into my house and to my kitchen making sure my adopted sister didn't catch me otherwise I would be dead. As I stepped in the kitchen I saw my brothers discussing who would have the last piece of chocolate cake. Problem solved.

As I was going to be a spy I had to practise so while they were distracted I snuck up on both my brothers, I stretched my arm to touch the cake then I heard, "Oi!" It was a familiar voice. Before anything happened, I dropped the chocolate cake and ran...

Katie Mantke (10)

St Joseph's Catholic Primary School, Redhill

A Day In A Spy's Life

An extract

Dear Diary,

Today I was trapped in eternal pain for like, a lifetime. My body is still really stiff and bruised, unlike how flexible I usually am. I know what you're thinking, how in the world does a ten-year-old girl, by the name of KC Chime, possibly manage to get themself into such a deep hole? If I'm honest with you, I'm not really sure. One second I'm in school living a very ordinary life and the next I am out fighting crime. Life just is not the same. Unlike any other mission, this one almost cost me my very own life and probably much more in some way.

So, like usual, me and my siblings were casually strolling off to our school, St Joseph's. We were thinking about what our next mission could possibly be. Then it hit me. Dad, our boss, said to expect a lot, that this might even go on for more than a month. Keep in mind that our missions usually take a day or less. He was serious. This was important on so many different levels.

"We need to confront Mr Pullar about this and Mr Edwards," I said.

Of course, they reluctantly agreed. Leading four siblings is pretty easy, I'm not gonna lie. After finally walking through the colossal gates of school my siblings glared at me. They knew that everything I did was paramount for success on the mission.

Mr Pullar was waiting patiently, watching the door closely. We figured he was waiting for us. It was unlike him to be on his own on a day like this with such nice weather.

As we approached him, he quickly pulled us aside. KC, Amanda, Hailey, Alex David. I need to tell you about the newest gadgets to help you on your latest mission. Follow me."

Chikuzierem Chime (10)

St Joseph's Catholic Primary School, Redhill

Tuesday 27th August 2009

An extract

Dear Diary,

You know, stalking people may sound like an easy task, but it's not. The main reason being you don't want to be caught and get fired.

My last task sent me to the hospital for weeks and I'm still here. This all happened because of my so-called friend, Jeffrey, who kidnapped my girlfriend and stabbed me. Just to add by the time anyone finds and reads this, I'll be long gone.

It was only today I got told I won't have much more time to live. Right, I'm going to explain my fatal story now. I wouldn't sit back and relax, this story will keep you on the edge of your seat the whole time.

So what happened was my so-called friend and I were walking to school one day when my watch started beeping and I knew I was needed. I told Jeffrey I saw something down the street and went to check it out. I ignored Jeffrey's questions and left. If you don't know that was a distraction so I could go to HQ.

After a few minutes of walking, I'd reached a calm and silent road. I looked around to check if the coast was clear.

When I knew for certain I was the only one around, I opened the hatch to a specific pothole and jumped in. Normally, you'd see a tunnel with muck in it but this tunnel was painted white with paintings of the association's most heroic spies who died in missions. Little did I know I would end up on that wall.

Out of nowhere, a voice boomed explaining about the kidnapping that took place in Zandvoort, Netherlands at 9:45pm approximately. The voice gave me information on the kidnapper.

A picture was placed in my hand and I recognised her as my girlfriend...

Max Brown (11)
St Joseph's Catholic Primary School, Redhill

Diary Of A Smart Kid

An extract

Dear Diary,

Somehow, today started normally. I walked to school. An unusual autumn breeze floated through my black hair.

I arrived at school ten minutes early. It was just enough time to finish all my work for today. Suddenly, I heard a notification from my phone. I went through my checklist. Did I do my homework? Did I make my bed? When I read the message my heart skipped a beat. NASA, the place my father worked had asked me to design Apollo 42. It was a dream come true but soon it would turn into my worst nightmare.

I walked back through the school gates. Ten minutes later, I was standing outside the mighty blue NASA building. Then I remembered something. Dad, after his flight to the moon, would design Apollo 42. I entered to find my dad's boss. He led me to his office and asked me, "Can you design Apollo 42?"

I replied, "Isn't that my dad's job?"

Dad's boss looked like he would cry. He replied, "That rocket flew off track."

He told me that my rocket's mission was to fly and save my dad's rocket and go to Mars. He led me to my office. I started sketching and labelling ten hours non-stop. I drew every pipe, every switch, every button until my fingers felt like they would fall off.

Finally, I'd finished my masterpiece. My dad depended on me. The fear that I'd messed up haunted me. The rocket was built so quickly you could say Mississippi and it was built.

I held my breath. It all came down to this. The countdown started, "Three... two... one... blast off!" The rocket flew off the floor and into the night sky...

Sebastian Watson (9)

St Joseph's Catholic Primary School, Redhill

My Diary

An extract

Dear Diary,

Today was a big disaster, I'm going to be miserable my whole life. I woke up feeling tired. Suddenly, I heard knocking on my bedroom door. I thought it was my sisters calling me to go downstairs but it turns out it was my very annoying older brother.

"Sis! Sis! I have good news to tell you!" I knew it was my brother. I recognise his voice anywhere. Suddenly, my brother slammed the door open without my permission and shouted, "Sis! Sis! You won't believe it! I'm going back to your academy!" How in the world is that good news?

I forgot to tell you that I lead a whole spy academy with no staff. I'm Mckayla and I'm thirteen years old. I know what you're thinking. I'm way too young to lead a spy academy for talented people. No offence to my brother but to me, he is not talented. He shouldn't have gone to my academy in the first place. Once, he wanted to prove he was talented enough to go on a mission with me but we almost got killed because of him.

Anyway, working at an academy is not the only thing I do. When I was eleven, I started helping Year 6 with their SATs at St Joseph's school. SATs are beginning soon, I had to go quickly so I still had time to help them before they started.

I grabbed my keys and opened my spy academy. Everyone came rushing in including my brother. It was unusual that he was excited to go to my academy. I thought we hated each other. Oh, I just remembered, the last time he came into my academy I banned him.

It's like he forgot! I can't believe I'm saying this... I gave him one more chance.

Sara Oliveira (10)

St Joseph's Catholic Primary School, Redhill

My Diary

An extract

Dear Diary,

Today was the most chaotic day of my life. My knees are aching, my hands are trembling and as you can probably already tell, I feel exhausted! Now, you're most likely to be wondering how the heck could a twelve-year-old go through such a frightening day and still survive. Well, you're about to find out...

It started like a normal Friday after school. My friends, Isla and Liana, had come over to game. We played lots of games such as Pac-Man and many others. At this time, we were playing Pac-Man. Strangely, all the characters had disappeared. We all thought that it was a glitch but it wasn't because the next moment, we weren't in my house sitting on the couch anymore. We had teleported somewhere else...

Liana, Isla and I were wondering where we were until we saw four ghosts appear. We looked around and realised that we were inside the game. Suddenly, we heard a voice that sounded like Bil. "Welcome to Pac-Man. I expect you to already know the rules but there are a few things I need to tell you.

You will have three lives. If you lose all three then you will die. You also have to get 400 points or you will also die!"

We all started to scream like crazy.

He started speaking again, "Five, four, three, two, one. Go!"

Suddenly, Liana teleported to the start of the game and the game started. She started to look for a circle but she just couldn't find one.

Alarmingly, two ghosts cornered Linana and caught her. We had just lost a life meaning we only had two lives left. We all started to panic...

Maria Joby (10)

St Joseph's Catholic Primary School, Redhill

Friday 25th July 2023

An extract

Dear Diary,

These past weeks have been crazy. You know how I wrote last week that we were moving to England? Well, that happened.

We were living in this small cabin but we didn't stay there for long. I complained to my mum about the cabin but she ignored me.

We lived in the UK for about a month. The whole reason we moved was because we got caught being spies. This was our shortest stay yet. Our family was so rich but we lived in small ugly houses and hotels. Even though we moved, I do feel guilty about the near-death experience this week. Let me tell you more...

After what seemed like a whole year, it was lunchtime. I bumped into my brother coming out of the lunch hall, crying his eyes out. I walked into the lunch hall...

"Look! There's the other spy kid!"

Everyone started laughing. I dropped my lunch and ran to my brother.

"How did they find out?" asked my brother.

I didn't answer.

It was my friends.

Me and my brother left school upset. My brother was sick to the bottom of his stomach. I felt so bad. My mum was packing up all our stuff. We entered the house and my mum said, "We're moving to Liverpool, a new city."

I started helping my mum pack and we were in the car by 4pm. I liked this town, but I hope it didn't happen again.

I actually got some sleep in the car and we finally arrived in our new town. Mum found a fancy hotel room for us. When I got out of the car and walked down the street to the hotel, it felt like a walk of shame. I felt so guilty...

Grace Edland (11)

St Joseph's Catholic Primary School, Redhill

The Incredible Diary Of Cerberus

An extract

Dear Diary,

Sorry if I made you worried. I was so caught up when Hades recruited me and I became a... Let me tell you what happened.

I was on a daily troll in the Underworld when I uncovered a conversation. I turned back to leave until they said my name so I stayed.

"Oh, I heard Cerberus will be given an offer to join."

"Cerberus will soon join Hades in work."

At first, their words confused my brain until I realised what they meant. I jumped in excitement as my dream would come true.

They were right, as Hades' undead knight came up to me to ask me to visit Hades. I jumped up and down, almost breaking the floor. It had been a millennium since people came to the palace so it's very important.

As I entered the throne room, Hades sat on the throne menacingly as he glared in a serious manner.

"I have gathered you for an offer."

As I asked what the offer was, he gave me a task in return for being a helper.

"You have to collect a hundred souls."

You may think this would be easy as I'm a demon hound but I don't have experience catching souls. A demon recommended a reaper scythe. At that point, I needed it if I wanted it to work so I asked him and he gave it to me. He said to keep it. Then he left but I forgot to ask him how it worked. I saw a soul and I slashed and collected it.

I kept repeating that to get all the souls. I randomly got transported to the place and I gave all the souls to Hades. He accepted them and now I'm working, my dream.

Avaanesh Arruran (11)

St Joseph's Catholic Primary School, Redhill

The Incredible Diary Of A Spy

An extract

Dear Diary,
You can't imagine the day I've had. I was sent on the most terrifying mission of my life. I had to go to Antarctica. Imagine how I felt when I was told I had to travel across the world. Did they really think that I was the best man for the job?

It all started when I began fighting one of the villains of the week. Usually, they were more experienced and better fighters but today I was far superior. They had new weapons and didn't seem to be able to use them effectively. Suddenly, without warning, we fell into a power plant. I couldn't believe my eyes. I had returned to the place of my first mission. Looking around, I saw, to my surprise, that the power plant had been annihilated. It dawned on me that the villain of the week was one of the scientists who had worked on the project. I saw him holding a piece of the power plant which crumbled in his hand. Suddenly, he charged at me. If he touched me it would be game over for me but he tripped into the reactor core which was very anticlimatic. *Well, better get on with my mission,* I thought as I hurried away. As the wind hit my face I knew that this was going to be a difficult task.

As I arrived at the eerie cave an eerie shiver went down my spine. *Man up, this is a mission just like any other!* I thought to myself. Slowly, I secured the important weapons and crept towards the exit. Normally it isn't that easy to take such high-tech weapons. As I stepped outside a giant avalanche came raining upon me.

Raphael Adetunji (11)

St Joseph's Catholic Primary School, Redhill

The Journal Of Chris The Camera

An extract

Dear Diary,

What a week it's been. The toys in the box with me were unusually chatty. They hadn't been this chatty since that toy Ferrari swallowed that fly. I was getting bored of all the nonsense that all the chatty toys had to say. I wanted to see the world! I also wanted to take pictures of all the incredible sites like Africa, the tallest skyscrapers and many other landmarks. Not just fashion icons like Dazzle the unicorn plushy. Horrible!

I was having an amazing thirty-minute nap. Proud! The only good thing that you can do around these parts! But I was rudely interrupted by some loud customer footsteps. Where can you ever find quiet? The annoying customer entered the shop and sprinted right up to me. I was ready to charge! He started swiping and poking my buttons and screen. It was very annoying. Gosh! Why me? Eventually, after staring at my face for about an hour, he placed me on this counter and put £90 worth of coins on it. Weird!

Anyway, he took me on this giant vehicle with wings. What for? It was so boring! All I did was sit there, doing nothing for ten hours. Once we finally landed, me and my owner, David Attenborough, went to this giant zoo-looking place full of animals. What a pickle I was in. David Attenborough started to press the capture button more than 100 times. After three hours of this torture, we finally got to chill in this luxury resort.

I was exhausted. But I was scared about what was going to happen tomorrow...

Leonardo Santin (10)
St Joseph's Catholic Primary School, Redhill

The Twelve-Year-Old Spy

Dear Diary,

I am in shock. This was the worst day ever. I got awoken at six in the morning to go on a school trip I didn't want to go on. Not only that but I couldn't even sleep on the bus because the kids in the back of the bus were screaming and wailing.

Once we got there, I couldn't have fun because they called me and told me a ten-year-old had been kidnapped. I was extremely worried about the child getting hurt so I told my teacher I needed the toilet and rushed to the address my boss sent me.

Once I got there I knocked on the door. But there was no one there. I ran around the house but still, it took me a long time to think about the creepy basement. It was dark, spooky, and scary but I continued walking down the steps.

Suddenly, I spotted the child and kidnapper. I got handcuffs. The kidnapper got the child out safely. I was glad that I was locking the kidnapper away. Suddenly, I realised I hadn't put the handcuffs on properly and he ran away.

I ran after him but after I turned the corner, he was gone, Then suddenly, I saw an abandoned shop. I went inside and scanned the room.

I saw the kidnapper with his short, silky brown hair and jet-black mask. I slowly crept towards him and trapped him in handcuffs.

I took him to the police station and he yelled, "Let me go!"

The police locked him up. I walked out of the police station and my boss called me to thank me and then I went back to my class.

Narayah Andrews-Green (9)

St Joseph's Catholic Primary School, Redhill

Nyla... Horror

An extract

Dear Diary,

I was sitting in my bed. I had a very big house. I was watching my tablet. It was ten o'clock. I was relaxing when I saw something at my window. I saw a man watching and staring at me. He looked quite old. The man was smiling. It was creepy. I screamed and my dad opened the door. He saw the man too. The man ran away and Dad called someone.

The next day, I was returning from school with my friend, Polina. We were going to the park. We did so many fun things. Polina's mum called and told her to go home. Pilina hugged me like last time and left me alone...

I was sure that I wouldn't want to go home because of that man. I was thinking about it. There were more people in the park but it was getting darker. The people started to head home. It was like something was scaring them.

I heard the sound of my phone ringing. It was my dad. He sounded different. He told me to go home and I said okay. I started to go home. I heard the sound again. It was my dad again but it wasn't.

He turned around and I saw the man from the day before. I started to go farther and he started to go faster. This made me scream. "Argh! What do you want?"

The men started to run. Then he screamed, "Come here!" It sounded like something not real. It sounded like a horror film.

I saw a forest and thought the man had lost her. She ran off to the forest...

Polina Maeyr (10)
St Joseph's Catholic Primary School, Redhill

The Adopted Family...

An extract

Dear Diary,

The mission that I had was crazy and especially when they recruited a twelve-year-old boy from St Bede's school. I was two years older than him but then, he took the practise course. He straight away said that this was too 'easy' for him.

When we got to the hiking mission, he immediately got a branch and threw it at them but I was in my hiding spot so they only saw him. As they were chasing him, I got to the mission. I found the secret book of missions and their map. I got back into my hiding spot and saw him run to me. I pulled him into the hiding spot. I told him to be very quiet and he was but not until we ran back. He had so many questions for me. He asked me to tell him my secret, about how I made it out without a single scratch. I told him how I have been trained to know every single mission. He then went to his room and so did I.

I thought to myself for a moment. Then I told myself out loud that he was alright. That's the first time I'd said that anyone was alright. I told the general and he was amazed that I said so.

He wanted me to take him in my team. I told him that I didn't care if he was in my team or not. I just wanted him to be trained in all of the missions. Tomorrow things were different, very different. I was getting adopted, along with the twelve-year-old boy I now knew and that was a big problem...

Lily-May Wicker (10)
St Joseph's Catholic Primary School, Redhill

Tragic Holiday

An extract

Dear Diary,

I still can't believe I'm writing this. It's a story I can't believe but it happened. I've never been so frightened, it's actually crazy. I think my ear is still clogged with water and I'm getting goosebumps from just writing about this.

It all started when me and Dylan were going on a plane to Poland. Don't get me wrong, I love travelling but this took a big turn... We went through security and got on the plane normally. Nothing went wrong except Dylan was a bit homesick and travel sick but overall it was pretty normal and peaceful.

Then it started shaking. I told myself it was just turbulence but we were in the middle of the flight. I rocked myself from side to side. I tried to wake Dylan up. After a few seconds, he woke up and to no surprise, he was terrified. Then I felt my heart drop down to my stomach and pow! we crashed into the sea.

I didn't think I would make it out and I don't even know how, but I was extremely nervous. Dylan was unconscious.

"I'm only fourteen, I can't die!" I shouted.

Dylan then woke up. My lip was bleeding and he was bleeding too. The pilot was coughing out blood as the water was rising. It was up to my shoulders.

"We have to get out," Dylan barked.

Do you think we got out?

Natalia Rusilowska (11)

St Joseph's Catholic Primary School, Redhill

Superhero

Dear Diary,

I've never had an opportunity in my life. My chest is still beating and my knees are still oozing with blood and my knuckles have blisters. I know what you're thinking, how does a ten-year-old girl from primary school get recruited by MI13 for a top mission? The mission I shouldn't talk about almost cost me my life.

My day started like every other pointless day. The alarm rang and stung my ears like a hornet piercing venom into my skin. As I wiped the sleep out of my eyes, I hammered the password into the phone and deactivated the alarm. My body slowly adapted to the rising sun as I flopped out of bed. I went downstairs and all of a sudden...

Beep! I got a clue from my watch saying: 'You need to get to the park. A girl has been captured by Smithy Smith'. I ran to the park to find the girl. All of a sudden, I saw her screaming, "Argh!" I rushed over but the man ran away. I ran as fast as I could. I felt so scared. I called my friend, Nyla. *Ring! Ring!* "Nyla, I need you!"

Nyla ran as fast as she could. "I need your freeze power!"

Nyla froze the bad guy and went to get the girl. Then my watch flew out a green badge and the girl lived in no danger again.

Nyla Funge (11)
St Joseph's Catholic Primary School, Redhill

The Incredible Diary Of The Bully's Pencil

Dear Diary,

Today was the worst! My lead is broken and my rubber is aching just like every other day. I'm the only pencil owned by the bully. I don't even want to be owned, especially by the bully. All people do is stare. They don't even need to talk to say that I'm a weirdo because their facial expressions show it. Before today even happened, I was living my best life but I guess there are good and bad days and I guess today was one of them.

A couple of weeks ago, I was clueless about where I was but I soon found out I was lost under the homework books. Well, of course, the bully had forgotten about me because that's how he is... careless. I've tried multiple times to make him not pick on people at school.

All of a sudden, an idea popped into my head. I needed to find his homework book. But, of course, he hadn't done it. So I looked for a piece of paper. Coincidentally, there was a piece of paper.

I wrote a sentence saying: 'Why are you bullying? Why not do some good?'
He finally changed.

Jamie Pettitt (9)
St Joseph's Catholic Primary School, Redhill

My Diary

Dear Diary,

Today was the craziest day ever. My YouTuber friend was using me, Then my percentage ran out. He put me on charge and then somehow he lost me. Bro, I was fuming, that's like the fifth or sixth time this month!

Bro, I just realised what happens if no one finds me. And where am I? I screamed as someone picked me up. It wasn't my original owner. Before you ask, I don't know who picked me up.

His face told me he'd hit the jackpot. He knew I was worth like two grand at least because I am an old vintage camera in good condition. My original owner lost me five or six times and dropped me at least fifty times in two to three weeks. That's ridiculous.

I think my new owner is MrBeast or something. I'm so lucky and I haven't been dropped yet. Hopefully, he doesn't replace me because he has lots of money. Bro, I'm sorry. Got to go, for now, my owner is about to use me for a video. At least we managed to catch up. See you. Speak to you tomorrow.

Alfie Pettit

St Joseph's Catholic Primary School, Redhill

A Day In The Life Of A Mario Hater

Dear Diary,

Today I failed once again. He was launched out of a cannon but Mario is too powerful! In the evening I went for a Mario Kart race and I was about to cross the line and come first but my brother threw a red shell at me and I came *last* instead. I was so frustrated but maybe tomorrow...

Alfred Ward (9)

St Julian's Church School, Wellow

Cricket Ball

Dear Diary,
I was hit by something. It hit me. I went too far and it was a 6. England won the 3rd test match and won the Ashes and the crowd roared. It was the best day ever.

Harrison Lord (9)
St Julian's Church School, Wellow

A Day In The Life Of A Teacher

Dear Diary,

I had a very stressful day. First, I had to teach twenty-one students about diary entries. One wrote about cats. Once they all finished their work, it was breaktime. For my snack, I had an apple and coffee.

After break, I let them have five more minutes to work. One of them told me that they were making a diary for me.

At the end of the day, I finally had some quiet time. From Miss Gillen.

Jood Ahmed (8)

St Malachy's Primary School, Belfast

The Foolish Flies Of South East Asia

I, Finogun, was flying around Bush Island in South East Asia with my mates when we saw a human called Kai. Kai looked nice and friendly and was on the phone. It seemed like he was going to go to the Isle of House on the coast of Myanmar and we were in Indonesia. My friends didn't want to go there because apparently that is where humans live but I was so eager. I made them a deal that they could not decline. "If we go to the Isle of House I promise you, I will never let you go outside of Bush Island."

They agreed and so we went. We travelled for what seemed like 100 miles.

Finally, after hours, we arrived at the Isle of House. We snuck in and saw it was almost deserted until we came upon the living room. It was full of people and they saw us appear from the kitchen so they brought the bug zapper out so we split up and flew for our lives.

When we were about to exit, the zapper zapped Ryan. We could do nothing but leave the house, then in the blink of an eye I got stuck in a web. My friends tried to pull me out but the spider got to me and grabbed me. Out of nowhere a cockroach came and scared off the spider and took us home.

When we arrived home I told my mum and dad and they quarantined us for the rest of my life.

Kazi Ullah (11)

St Mary's Catholic Primary School, Loughborough

The FIFA Mobile Virus

Dear Diary,
One day Rocker, Niblo 2, Punkdude and I were playing FIFA Mobile when we were sucked into our iPads. We looked at our teams and saw bronze players, but I had 115 Haaland from PL TOTS. We played PL TOTS and got Trippier. On Bundesliga we got Kobel 110 and on LaLiga we got Valverde and I sold all of them and got the UTOTS team.
From Sad.

Sammy Dalby (9)
St Mary's Hampton CE Primary School, Hampton

212

Diary Of A Hamster

Dear Diary,

I'm Whiskers the Hamster and this is my diary.

I started out in a cage. I needed to get out.

Someone picked me up and put me in a ball.

Before the lid was put on, I jumped out and ran away.

I found myself in a maze of feet. I ran but fell into a drain. I wanted to go back home. So I did. I jumped on a pipe and got out of the drain, through the foot maze and through the letter box back to my cage. Then I went to sleep.

Oliver Davidson (9)

St Mary's RC Primary School, Edinburgh

A Day In The Life Of A Frog

Dear Diary,

Today I woke up with a big ribbit. I had a big night of getting bugs for dinner but it was a good night. Sleep now.

I had breakfast and I went to the gym. First I hopped from lilypad to lilypad twenty times. Then I lifted some lilypads. Then I went home.

I had lunch on the pond and relaxed for the next hour. After that, I had a swim for thirty minutes and then had dinner.

I went to bed and had a beautiful dream.

Giorgia Pratico (10)

St Mary's RC Primary School, Edinburgh

The Incredible Diary Of Amelia Earhart

Featuring a quote from 'Good Night Stories for Rebel Girls'

Dear Diary,

I can't possibly express how I'm feeling right now. It is ten minutes till take-off for my mission to become the first woman to fly around the world. All my past adventures aboard my beloved Canary have been building up to this. I know I can do this and with my love of aviation and the woman of the world behind me, I know I can achieve the impossible.

Dear Diary,

Currently, we are flying over the Pacific Ocean and our engine is failing. Robert (my navigator) and I know that we'd be lucky to have another day. It has been two months since we set off from California and are on our last leg. It is important that when I'm gone people remember that 'I am quite aware of the hazards. I want to do it, because I want to do it. Women must try to do the same things that men have tried. If they fail, their failure must be a challenge to others'.

I've seen some amazing things, I just wish I could live to tell the tale.

May Reynolds (9)

St Paul's CE Primary School, Leamington Spa

The Lost Girl

Dear Diary,

My name is Crystal. One time I got lost so I'm here to tell you about it. This all began on Sunday. I was at a market with my mum and dad when I let go of their hand and when I looked for them they were gone. I was terrified, scared and sad. I didn't know where my parents were. I was looking for hours, days and nights and they still were nowhere to be found. Would I ever find them? That was how it all happened but I'm back with my parents now safe at home. We have never trusted that market ever since but I'm just glad I'm with my parents now. One thing that you need to remember is that your parents are always with you and it doesn't matter if they're in the world or if they're with God.

Anyway, I need to go now. See you soon.

Sincerely,

Crystal.

Summer Taylor (10)
St Sebastian's RC Primary School, Douglas Green

The Magnificent Diary Of Alicia Johnson

Dear Diary,

Tomorrow is the big day. I have a baseball match tomorrow and I've got everything (and I mean everything) prepared.

I packed water (to keep me hydrated), snacks (healthy nuts) to keep me up and about, my bat and my ball.

Today I couldn't find my equipment! Where had it gone? Little did I know that Felix the troublesome cat had hidden my equipment! Today was the match. I was so worried that I wouldn't find my equipment before the match! My family helped me find my equipment. Finally, we found it! It was behind the standing television. My brother, Leo, found it there. My mother scolded Felix (well, a cat doesn't understand human language so I didn't see the point). I am very glad.

Davia Okon (10)

St Sebastian's RC Primary School, Douglas Green

Incredible Cookie Diary

Dear Diary,

Today was the worst day ever! So, some lady picked me up and took a huge bite out of my head. Oh, I got really angry but she said I was really delicious. The worker said, "Only because you are in Tesco's dessert shop." The lady agreed.

Later that day, I was so confused because I was burnt but tasty. I was in so much pain. I just felt a bit ungrateful, but I don't know.

After that, I still couldn't figure out how ungrateful I am. I'm still in pain. Still, at least I am still alive. Just missing a big chunk out of my head. So much pain. Bye for now!

Lilly Edwards (10)

St Thomas More Catholic Primary School, Cheltenham

The Incredible Diary Of A Photo

Dear Diary,

Today has been annoying. I have tried to get past the firewall, yet have failed. So I am still stuck on the Samsung. The gallery is incredibly humongous. To be honest, it's quite sad actually.

I have tried and tried and failed. But hey, let's be positive. At least he hasn't moved me to the trash yet. Not yet. It is very lonely. Sometimes I hear the sound of Samsung's laugh. It goes, *ring-ring-ring!* There are nice holiday photos. I wish I was there, it looks like a lot of fun.

Kenzie Morris-Harker (10)

St Thomas More Catholic Primary School, Cheltenham

The Incredible Diary Of Hop The Rabbit

Dear Diary,

I've been in a cage since I can remember. I do not even like it. Tomorrow, I shall make my escape.

First, I will sleep if you don't mind.

Morning! I'm ready to escape but there is one tiny problem, I don't know how. Just let me think... Hmmm... Errr... Um... Great! I got it! I shall use my rope to play and use it as a Lasso. I'll get the keys for the cage, open it and jump off the balcony and escape.

I did just that and it worked. I was starving. I was wondering if the outside world had any food. I went to the shop and tried to ask for carrot cake but the humans didn't seem to understand me.

I miss my home and my owners. I don't think that the escape was a good idea. I'll just head back home. But how? Got it! I'll just go in the open door. It worked! I got back in, back in my small but safe cage. Now I know that the cage is much safer than the outside world.

Amelia Browarna (8)

St Thomas' Primary School, Riddrie

The Incredible Diary Of Gautroop

Dear Diary,

I am really dark blue and I can shape-shift into anything. I also cannot die. I found a hero who can go into the forbidden temple. It went so badly wrong!

He accidentally fell down a giant hole where there were friendly fairies that gave him the orb of Mabu. But it was a fake!

I stumbled across the fairies one day and they told me the story and took me back to the past and I found it myself. I stole the real orb of Mabu. Don't tell the fairies!

Matteo Del Rossi (8)

St Thomas' Primary School, Riddrie

The Incredible Diary Of Millie

Dear Diary,

Today I met my little cousin, Lucia. She was tiny in her pink little babygrow. We met her at my auntie's house. I got to hold her for the first time ever. I was crying happy tears. She was so cute. When I fed her her bottle she fell asleep in my arms. After, my mum said it was time to put her back in her bed. We stayed at my auntie's house. I loved seeing my little cousin, Lucia.

Millie Ward (9)
St Thomas' Primary School, Riddrie

The Incredible Diary Of Mr Monster

Dear Diary,

I was a human but I got turned into a purple monster. I called myself Mr Monster. I kinda liked being a purple monster but I don't know why I have fur. I'm a furry monster. I wear a top hat everywhere, every day. I haven't written how I got turned into a monster because I don't know how! I'm super close to finishing a device to turn me back into a human.

Aaron Murray (9)
St Thomas' Primary School, Riddrie

The Incredible Diary Of Erling Haaland

Dear Diary,

Today was a great day. I won the UCL. It started when we conceded two goals but I got a penalty and I scored in the top corner. The crowd went wild. All I could hear was, "Erling! Erling! Erling!" There were four minutes left. There was a free kick... and I scored. We had won the match and I lifted the trophy.

Olly Smith (9)

St Thomas' Primary School, Riddrie

Once A DJ

Dear Diary,

Today was crazy, I was in a rave (because that's my job) and all of a sudden I looked back at the crowd and everyone was gone! I couldn't believe what I was seeing, I was lost for words. So I went looking for them, I travelled all around Newcastle for ages. Finally, I found them. You will never guess where they were; *another rave!* I was fuming, outraged and most of all angry! I did ask someone why they all left, it was because they heard no music.

I was like, "Eh? I have no clue how you didn't hear the music."

I ran and ran and ran back to my rave and saw two people who I saw DJing at the other place (where everyone left me). *They were the ones turning my speakers off!* So ever since, I stopped being a DJ.

Maisie Walker (11)

Stanley Crook Primary School, Stanley

The Great Fire

3rd September 1666,

Dear Diary,

I was asleep when I smelt smoke coming from downstairs. I realised there was a fire, so I looked out of the casement window. I realised four houses beside me were in flames. Fire was ripping through the city.

I was panicking, so I grabbed my money and got the cart. I headed to the Thames. I got my boat out and away. I saw St Paul's Cathedral had caught on fire. I heard screaming. There were people using hoses to spray water at the fires. "Keep going!" shouted a man, commanding people pulling houses down to create a fire break. I then saw my house in flames.

Nathan Todd (8)

Strandtown Primary School, Belfast

The Great Fire Of London

Dear Diary,

I woke up at night and I heard people screaming and smelt smoke. It was a magnificent fire. People got water from the River Thames to put out the fire. People used gunpowder to blow up the houses. People used old fire engines to get the fire as well.

People were scared, sad, and feeling bad. People jumped out of their houses, but only six people died in the Great Fire of London. Lots of people died in the plagues.

The houses were beside each other so it was easy to spread the fire. The wind was not strong, so people grabbed water from the River Thames and the fire was gone.

Ashlin Vijeesh (8)

Strandtown Primary School, Belfast

The Great Fire

Dear Diary,

Today, I awoke to a strange glowing light at my bedroom window. I soon realised it was a crackling fire. I quickly jumped out of bed and woke my whole family. I said we needed to risk jumping out of the window. It took a couple of tries before they agreed. I was quite scared myself, but it was the only choice we had. So first my parents jumped, then my brother and I. We looked across the houses on my street, they were all either fully burnt down or very burnt. We barely escaped the fire while we were trying to get to the River Thames to flee London.

Norah Armstrong (8)
Strandtown Primary School, Belfast

My Incredible Diary

Dear Diary,

Willy Wonka went to a secret room and that room makes bubblegum. There was this girl called Violet and she was desperate to try the bubblegum. Not yet though.

"What's happening to Violet? Mr Wonka, may you help me? I told her not to eat it yet but she wouldn't listen. What should I do about it?"

"Okay, I will help you but she's going to be ill. Charlie, may you come with me?"

"Where am I going?"

"You're the winner. I may take you to a lovely place."

"Where is that place?"

"Let's go on the elevator."

Hajra Khan (8)

Sybourn Primary School, Waltham Forest

My Incredible Diary Of Charlie

Dear Diary,

I went to Mr Wonka's chocolate factory. It was magnificent! There was candy everywhere just like Candyland so I thought to myself, *is Mr Wonka made out of candy?* The entertainment was horrible, I almost burnt myself! Mr Wonka had luminous, silky brown hair and a suit that was purple and it looked like he was going to a funeral. We can't forget the stick, it looked worse than my grandad's! The cream is the cream room and it was the worst room ever. There was hair cream and whipped cream and how do you eat hair cream?

Izzabelle Madden (9)

Sybourn Primary School, Waltham Forest

The Incredible Diary

Dear Diary,
On the 9th of July, I was in the factory and there were so many candy canes as sweet as the chocolate river. There were also some very luscious sweets as scrumptious as the chocolate river. Then one kid loved the chocolate river and the chocolate and he kept on just slurping on all of the river non-stop. When he went for a very enormous slurp... *splash!* The poor boy slipped in the river. Everyone was as shocked as his mom. It was a good day after that but the chocolate river is haunted.

Ashar Syed
Sybourn Primary School, Waltham Forest

Freya The Fox's Diary

Dear Diary,

When I woke up I felt petrified. Today I had to go to the warden's castle to fight him. I mean, I'm just little, I'm only eight but I guess I have to. I was running on all four legs and I saw a deep, dark castle in front of me. I was feeling brave but knew I would lose the fight. Anyway, I knocked on the door but nobody answered so I rang the doorbell. Then the cage fell down on me and the warden marched to me and I was terrified. I thought he was going to help me but he didn't. I was left alone.

After a few hours he came back and said, "If you can beat me in a fight then you can go home but if I beat you I will keep you here!"

Two hours of fighting and I won. I went home to celebrate.

Freya Wallace (8)

Tarland Primary School, Tarland

The Princess Butterfly

Dear Diary,

I am the kindest buttefly princess ever. Even if someone hurts me I would say it's alright. One day though something didn't feel right. I went and bumped into my friends and I said, "Things don't seem right!"

Everyone said, "Yeah, it doesn't."

There was a thunderstorm suddenly in the middle of summer and one hour later the storm passed and it was all back to normal and dare I say it, we were happy.

Well, anyway, bye-bye.

Amber Pittendreigh (7)

Tarland Primary School, Tarland

My Surprising Day

Dear Diary,

Today was a very surprising day! Dad took me out on his boat called Catch-a-lot. Dad wanted to go whaling, I think he's addicted. But I did not. Off to the Atlantic Ocean I went.

I was rowing for what seemed like ages, an eternity. Then Dad ran to the other side of the boat for no reason. The waters were empty. Nothing. Not even a fish to catch. Then everything went all blurry.

Our seagull, Mr Squawksalots, looked at a whale's eye. It got scared and flew at Dad. I got out my lamp and looked into the ocean. Dad got back on. Out of nowhere, a huge storm started. I could barely row the boat. Then we got stuck in a tidal wave. Dad let go of the lamp and it flew away. The whale hit the boat and we went flying. Dad jumped off our boat. Our boat Catch-a-lot was falling apart. He grabbed the spear in mid-air and he stabbed the whale and killed it. The sky made me feel like I was in Heaven. It looked glorious. This was worth it.

Sam Holland (10)

The Wilmslow Academy, Cheshire

The Long Move

Dear Diary,

I've had a dreadful day tidying all my toys while my brother, my mum and my dad were loading up the Enterprise van ready for moving to Cornwall. What a move! Norfolk to Cornwall; I mean, a seven-hour drive, that's longer than a plane flight to Spain! My mum came in.

"Come on, Joey, let's go to Cornwall!"

We got into the car. I whispered, "Goodbye, old home!" We left.

Seven hours later, we arrived. We went inside slowly and lonely. I wonder what living here will be like?

From Joey.

James Sparkes (9)
Thompson Primary School, Thompson

Cristano's World Cup Win

Dear Diary,

In Qatar I woke up for the cup final, tired but excited. I put on my strip for the game, out my boots on and drove to the stadium in my Bugatti, revving the engine and bending the wheel.

The spaces were full and the stadium was loud. Coaches were all around the place. I ran in and got there just in time, got on the field and then... "Oh hell!" It was Messi. Then I realised Ángel Di María was there, it was Portugal versus Argentina, this was going to be a good game.

Kick-off began, the whistle blew, and a ball to Messi from the Argentinian striker. Ruben Diaz tackled Messi, foul! Free kick for Portugal. I scored the winning goal!

Euan Brown (9)

West Linton Primary School, West Linton

The Fight For Life, By Gandalf The White

Dear Diary,

I have had a long day of fighting the deadliest enemy I have yet had to face Durin's Bane, the Balrog of Moria.

I started the day in the dreary, abandoned and soulless halls of upper Moria. As me and The Fellowship (The Fellowship of the Ring) set out on our day's march, we came upon a room. Now this room wasn't any different from the others, we barricaded the doors as we had a break. Then as quick as lighting, a horde of goblins came down upon us! We ran for our lives! As we came upon a bridge the Balrog stood menacingly. Spells after spells raced through my head as I tried to recall one that would help. *Pop!* I had found the right spell! Convincingly, the words broke through the darkness. "You shall not pass!" I roared. Moments later, the Balrog tumbled into the depths under the bridge. Unluckily, the many-thonged whip the Balrog carried wrapped around my leg with a vice-like grip. After that, it felt like years falling down in the unending night. Finally, I landed at the bottom. Now came the fiery rage of the Balrog.

He was on the retreat, heading up the forgotten halls until we reached the endless stairs, when I lost sight of him.

When I finally reached the peak of Zirakzigil, his fire was reborn like a phoenix. We struggled in battle until I overcame the beast and threw him down to his fiery doom.

In the struggle, I lost most of my life force. Next thing I knew, I was being carried away by an eagle, back to Lothlórien, the realm of the healing, where I have been reborn as Gandalf the White, and that is where I'm writing to you now.

Theodore Hickling (10)

Westonbirt School, Tetbury

Coco's Diary

Dear Diary,

What a wagtastic day! I knew today was going to be great when I woke up to the mouth-watering smell of sausages. After breakfast, I got to go on a great big run with the kids on their bikes and I couldn't wait to explore! We ran with the kids and had a great time and then they turned a corner and stopped so we followed them and saw a gleaming river. As soon as I saw it I took a running leap and plunged into the deep, cool water. I was closely followed by Oscar, who made an even bigger splash than me! (Only because he's four years older than me, I'm one and a half and he's five and a half!). Then it was time to head back to our campsite.

Oscar and I trotted on ahead and eventually, after much panting and stopping, we reached the top of the hill. I blinked in surprise to see a baby donkey with massive ears and such a fluffy coat standing in front of me. He was very sad as he had lost his mum, but soon cheered up when Oscar and I used our super sniff sniffers to take him back to her. The children rewarded us with more sausages for dinner! Yum!

Isabel Nassif (10)
Westonbirt School, Tetbury

Year Two

Dear Diary,

Today was the last day of Warthogs, it's been a crazy year. I've been turned into a frog for sneaking out. I battled Medusa today, it was challenging but I used my wand to shoot her (hard when you're a frog).

I also crashed my friend Jake's car! My evil teacher (Epans) said I'm on my last chance!

Tomorrow I'm going to follow the mystical butterflies and dig up the evil centipede.

See you tomorrow.

Ryan.

Ryan Dodd (10)

Whitchurch CE Junior School, Whitchurch

Anne Frank's Diary (In My Own Words)

Day 1

Dear Diary,

Hello, I am Anne Frank. I was born in the German city of Frankfurt. This is the diary I wrote while hiding from the Nazis. My sister Margot is three years older than me. She is currently a senior and is hiding with me. Hitler hates the Jews and blames us for all the country's problems. The hatred of the Jews and the poor economic situation made my parents (Edith and Otto Frank) decide to move to Amsterdam. There my dad founded a gelling agent for making jam.

This is my first day of hiding from the Nazis. I'm scared, we all are. I can't move, I'm still cautious that they may come... the Nazis.

Day 2

Dear Diary,

It has been announced that the Nazis will be doing daily checks in case people are going into hiding. My blood is turning cold. Why is Hitler like this?

Day 762

Dear Diary,

We haven't been found out yet and I'm getting more comfortable with my 'new home'. We have to stay here until the war's over... if the Nazis don't get us.

Day 763

Dear Diary,

I'm feeling good about this new place that's meant to be home. I haven't heard Nazi gunshots in a while. Oh no, they're coming in. We have to be silent. They have found our secret corridor. Oh no! Help. "Goodbye Kitty."

Neve Powell (10)

Whitleigh Community Primary School, Whitleigh

Vampire School

Dear Diary,
My name is Basil and I swear, yesterday it felt like there was something wrong with my school. All my teachers had giant canine teeth and were making us learn about different types of blood. That's why I'm trying to fake being sick so I don't have to go to my freaky, scary, weird school. Oh, my mums are coming, they're not going to get tricked so I better just go to school. I'm writing at school and I'm scared so I'll just...
"Hello darling, please can I see your blood?"
Help!

Lucia Sulley-Valent (10)
Windlesham School & Nursery, Brighton

The Discovery

Dear Diary,

One day me and my friend were walking in the park when we saw a tiny, strange creature which neither of us had seen before. We didn't know what to do. We got our phones out and tried to learn some stuff about the creature, but we couldn't find anything so we thought we had found a new creature. We phoned someone about the discovery. They said we could name it and while we were they would come look at the animal. We came up with a name and that was my favourite day!

James Wadsworth (10)
Windlesham School & Nursery, Brighton

Beatles

Dear Diary,

My name is Hermione and, well, I was too lazy to start on a Monday so today was Tuesday and all of a sudden I met the Beatles! For those who don't know who the Beatles are, shame on you! The thing is that I met Hey Jude and he said hey back. Also the Beatles introduced me to Lucy in the sky with diamonds, and, well, that was magnificent! When you meet someone you adore, make sure that they adore you too. Oh, one more thing: keep smiling and you will be happy.

Hermione Hawley (10)

Windlesham School & Nursery, Brighton

The Angry Guy's Great Escape

Dear Diary,

Yesterday I was with my table in my Year 5 classroom (which is the noisiest and worst class in the world) and all you ever hear is yay, woo, *ring!* So you know what I have to deal with. That's not the worst. It's after school. Yeah, you heard it. When the dreaded cleaner comes and does his job, eliminating me! But that won't happen this time because I built a bike so I can get away quickly. I may have a chance, that's if I survive. I will have my name on a big sign. Cool, isn't it? But when I was running the cleaner struck...

Archie Brown (9)

Winscombe Primary School, Winscombe

Thor's Reckless War

Dear Diary,

It was another exhausting day with sorrow and murder. I woke up in my wooden bed with a bad back. As soon as my eyes opened, my slaves came to give me breakfast (dagmal) which consisted of meat, fish and fruits (normally leftovers). To make my fascinating food they used a couldrum. I got out of bed in my linen underwear. Quickly, I hoovered up my food and put my clothes on. I threw my shoes on and got ready for war. As quick as a flash, I gathered my army and we headed off from my Thorsome castle!

There were at least eight longships with fifty men on each one! After a few hours, we arrived at Skullbone Forest in England. Suddenly, there were screams as the English fellows knew we had arrived. I thought my ears were going to fall off! We all ran and screamed, "Charge!" England's army ran towards us with hate, they really wanted to murder us. Blood splashed in the air as each warrior fell to the ground.

With rapid speed a knife went through my back, I punched the enemy in the face. My men took me back to the ship.

I was so vexed and full of disappointment and we went home. My army helped me and I went to my room with my dad and got life-saving treatment from my slaves.
Goodbye.

Elijah Ajala (10)
Woodlands School, Great Warley

Odin's Great Fall

Dear Diary,

Today, I have had a really tough time getting along with my two sons, Thor and Loki. I wanted to do something with Loki, so I shouted to him, "Loki!" I told him we could go hunting and luckily he said yes. So we set off.

When we got to the enchanted forest everything went dead silent for a moment or two and then out of nowhere a beastly wolf came and leapt onto Loki's leg. But before the wolf could get him I shot it and Loki and I were safe.

We next went to our longship to get back home. We both saw another ship and to my surprise, it was my mortal enemy Zeus (god of Greek mythology). I dusked down hoping he wouldn't see me, but he did. But we passed them with huge relief and we were two minutes away from home when we saw this bloodthirsty garmr. I forgot Thor was in the house alone but he had his magical hammer Mjölnir, but it wasn't enough. He died and I knew Zeus did it because the garmr was Zeus' pet, so I decided to give him a taste of his own medicine...

Teddy Spurling (10)
Woodlands School, Great Warley

The Magical Journey Of Thor Getting His Hammer

Dear Diary,

On a rainy evening in Asgard, I was training with a toy bow and arrow. I got bullied because I did not have a more powerful weapon. All the bullies had gone through real battles, but I had not.

I wanted to prove that I was brave, so I said, "Ask me anything and I will do it." I don't know why I said that. The leader of the bullies said, "Go in the forest that the Viking never came out of and still has not." I did not tell my dad Odin.

The next day, I went in the forest, it was daytime, but in the forest it was dark. Halfway in, I saw a man and realised it was the lost Viking. He tried to lift up a hammer, but he could not so I tried to pick it up and I started to fly! I picked up the Viking and flew straight through the top of the forest.

My dad was so proud! I've got to go and train with my hammer, bye!

Toby Ajala (8)

Woodlands School, Great Warley

Li'l Petey's Diary

Dear Diary,

This year hasn't been great. It started like this... So I got abandoned by my papa. He tried to make me evil like him but it didn't work. So he tried everything he could but it *still* didn't work. And a couple of days later he started to get sick of me. That day he left me outside a dog's house. Instead of it being an actual dog, it was a dog-headed cop. So what it was, was a policeman's body with a dog's head. The type of dog was a golden retriever. He loved me ever since I got there.

A couple of months later, I started making a robot called 80-HD and when he was built we made a big family (well, not that big). As we grew up we started dressing up as characters. Dog Man was Bark Knight, I was Cat Kid and 80-HD was Lightning Dude. When bad guys were out and about, we had to stop them.

As I grew up even more, my papa started to become nice. When everyone knew that he was a good guy they didn't put him in cat jail. I started to see him more. Now I have two families that love me. I am very happy and joyful. I go to my papa's in the week and on the weekends I go to Dog Man and 80-HD's.

Speak soon,
Li'l Petey.

Brooke Tomlinson (9)

Woodsetts Primary School, Woodsetts

Dog Man And The Crime Of The Bad Guy

Dear Diary,

You won't believe what happened today, it was crazy. Today I was playing with my friends in Sheffield so we thought it would be cool if we decided to go on top of a glass building and we saw a bad guy. I used my power of flight to catch him. After that, I jumped off the building and I fell off but the building smashed into pieces. Then I felt hurt, embarrassed, brave and fierce. I tried to fly and I flew for five seconds and fell flat on my face but then I went to get a coffee so I tried again and I could fly forever. After one minute I fought the evil man and I defeated him, so I did my victory dance, 'Orange Justice'.

That's my day, how is your day going?

From Dog Man.

Oliver Goodbold (9)

Woodsetts Primary School, Woodsetts

The Incredible Diary Of Candles

Dear Diary,

Today was extremely frantic and super crazy. It started off when I was having a chat with my friends, when suddenly I heard footsteps. I looked behind me and I saw a woman standing with a sharp-bladed knife ready to cut me and my friends up. I was scared and horrified but my friends were calm because they did not realise. When they finished singing we got cut up and my friends got eaten in a blink of an eye. So at this point I was left jumping out of my sponge. Then it was my turn to get put on the plate and get eaten. But to my surprise, I rolled off and smacked my face into my body. Then I got picked up again...

I hope I don't get eaten!

Speak soon,

Candles.

Poppy Dane (10)

Woodsetts Primary School, Woodsetts

Diary Of Flash

Dear Diary,

Today, I went on a walk. It took so long, but luckily I am fast so I started to run. I ran all the way to Subway and got a lovely Tuna Crunch sub. I felt like I was in Heaven because of how good it was. On the way home, I saw a stray dog. I took it home and went to the shop to get some dog food. I fed the food to the dog and called him Speedy because he is faster than me!

I wanted McDonald's, so I brought Speedy with me. But on the way there, on the path opposite me, I saw Spider-Man and he was seriously injured so I called an ambulance and told them what happened. They came right away and thankfully they came in time.

I got my food and I got Speedy a pup cup.

Millie May Jones (10)

Ysgol Bro Gwydir, Llanrwst

A Cow's Story

Dear Diary,

Today was the most intense day ever. I woke up and all of my friends, the other cows, were gone! I followed the trail of cow poo and, after a little while, I reached the other cows. They were on their way to another field. But what I didn't understand was why no one woke me up.

Then, four farmers took me to the shed and put me on the cattle-weighing scales. Then Farmer John said, "It's time. He's ready!" I had no idea what on Eerth was going on.

Right then, Farmer Mairy said, "Let's take him to the meat factory."

My heart skipped a beat. I knew that I had to leave, but how?

Nel Roberts (10)

Ysgol Bro Gwydir, Llanrwst

The Life Of A Ruler

Dear Diary,
Today has been atrocious for me. It has been rocky. People have been twisting me. People were playing catch with one another. They offended me. Later on, I got put into a big circular box. I carefully and quietly turned to see another of me, they said, "Oh, hi! What is your name?"
"I don't know."
"Well, mine is ruler, maybe that could be yours too?"
"Okay." I was scared to see another one of my kind. The girl was going to say something, then I got pulled out of the big circle. I was so sad! Suddenly, I got torn into pieces and thrown into the trash.

Jodi Jones (10)
Ysgol Bro Gwydir, Llanrwst

Principality Rugby

Dear Diary,

I play matches. Only in Principality, Wales National Rugby, but I'm in pain all the time. I'm kicked, thrown. I hate penalties. Players yell at me all the time. I feel sick when I hit the ground.

When I lose grip, that's a whole new story. After every game, I'm in pain. I say, "Why me? Why not another ball?" But I like going in the air if they catch me. In a scrum, I'm mad. If I land on the ground, I'm sad.

I go up the field with the players ramming, I go through so many. Two huge matches, France and New Zealand, they were hard matches. But we lost. I was annoyed.

Eban Jon Dafidd Roberts (10)

Ysgol Bro Gwydir, Llanrwst

Pencil Case

Dear Diary,

This morning, I was excited to go to school but I shouldn't have been. Today was horrific. People were treating me horribly, throwing me around, dropping me, stuffing pencils and all sorts in me. It was so annoying.

They treat me like nothing, I hate it so much. But when I got home, they were moving! And when they were moving, they left me behind. I thought they would come back, but they didn't. I was waiting for days but they sadly didn't come. Eventually, another family came and the girl that was in that family loved me, so she kept me. She took good care of me and I felt so nice.

Phoebe Parry Owen (10)

Ysgol Bro Gwydir, Llanrwst

The Dream

Dear Diary,

Yesterday was amazing, but very strange. I was in a dream! There were sweets everywhere - chewing gum, Skittles, Haribo, Maoam, Squashies, Sour Patch Kids, yummy!

I made new friends. We walked for ages. My feet started to hurt but then we found a banana split and we found a milk river! We took the banana split and rode it. It was like a boat. We sailed down the river. I drank some of the milk as well.

We finally arrived at our destination. We made a tent out of biscuits and we fell asleep, finally.

Efa Jones (10)
Ysgol Bro Gwydir, Llanrwst

Time Freeze Struck Again

Dear Diary,

This morning, I woke up. After that, the siren turned on. An emergency struck again and it was all my responsibility, so I changed quickly, rushed my breakfast, and then I was ready.

It was in the city, so I used my teleportation power to arrive early. It was my worst enemy: Time Freeze. His power is easy to understand, he freezes time. He can also freeze anything he wants to.

He was there, right in front of my eyes. But I was there to defeat him. Then he called in his sidekick.

Lela Mair Williams (9)

Ysgol Bro Gwydir, Llanrwst

Young Writers Information

We hope you have enjoyed reading this book – and that you will continue to in the coming years.

If you're the parent or family member of an enthusiastic poet or story writer, do visit our website **www.youngwriters.co.uk/subscribe** and sign up to receive news, competitions, writing challenges and tips, activities and much, much more! There's lots to keep budding writers motivated!

If you would like to order further copies of this book, or any of our other titles, then please give us a call or order via your online account.

Young Writers
Remus House
Coltsfoot Drive
Peterborough
PE2 9BF
(01733) 890066
info@youngwriters.co.uk

Join in the conversation!
Tips, news, giveaways and much more!

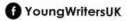 YoungWritersUK 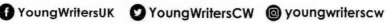 YoungWritersCW 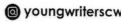 youngwriterscw

Scan me to watch The Incredible Diary Of video!